Carolina Blue
A Novella

Donn Weinholtz

Full Media Services

http://www.fullmediaservices.com

ISBN-13: 978-0-615-64908-5
ISBN-10: 0-615-64908-4

To Diane

"If you're at all like me, there are gonna be times when you need a little mind candy to make it through the academic year. When those times hit, find your way up to the Carolina Theater on Franklin Street and take in a movie. Or maybe this week, wander over to the Little Professor book store to pick up a shallow novel, or two, so you can treat yourself as needed."

Welcoming Remarks to New Graduate Students

– August 1972

Rev. Albert Murphy, Residence Director - Carlson Dorm
University of North Carolina – Chapel Hill

Contents

Chapter 1
Vladi

The forty-something Russian leaned against the dormitory's fourth-floor, balcony railing. He was practically naked and reveling in the late February sun. His ample belly folded over his black, spandex bikini. His thinning brown hair flowed to his shoulders. A fully–dressed, strawberry blonde, looking twenty years his junior, clutched his beefy arm.

Joe and I spotted him as we pulled into the Carlson Dorm parking lot with James Taylor's *Carolina in My Mind* blaring from the radio of my battered VW squareback. Looking up from the driver's seat, I lowered the radio's volume and registered my surprise.

"Whoa! Who's that up on my floor?"

"Got me, Eck. But he's payin' a stiff price for the fashion statement. It's about forty-two degrees out."

"Talk about crazy."

"Yeah, but look at the girl. The dude's doing something right. Maybe I'll get one of those streamlined bikinis. How do you think I'll look?"

"Like a low-rent, male stripper."

"Easy, Big Guy."

Joe, dripping sarcasm, often called me "Big Guy" even though I was 5'11" and about 150 pounds, while he was three inches taller and at least forty pounds heavier.

"If she's hanging all over him, with that blimp-like body; just think how she'll swoon for an Adonis like me."

"Dream on. You look like young Edmund Muskie with long hair and a gargantuan chin. Showing some skin isn't going to suddenly make you into a sex symbol."

"Well, little Eckhardt Larsen, will you ever stop taking cheap shots at my chin? How many times do I have to remind you that an exaggerated chin is the true indicator of virility? You're just jealous cause your stuck with an average chin and you're mired in a monogamous relationship - the only relationship that you've ever known. Meanwhile, a steady stream of enticing women keep coming on to me. "

He almost had me there. Over the years, so many women had treated me like their brother that I'd thought about becoming a priest.

"Ouch! low blow. But unlike you, Mr. Testosterone, I was never interested in cheap sex. There's a lot to be said for platonic relationships. Over the years, I've had some great female friends, and they provided the best training possible for a real relationship, a meaningful relationship. So, now I've got Olivia, while you're still dreaming of dressing up like a porn star in the hopes of landing yet another one night stand. So, you lose, I win; game, set, match Mr. Larsen."

This sort of jousting had gone on throughout our lives. Joe and I grew up together in Ocean City, New Jersey. We constantly tossed jibes at each other while in school, playing tennis, surfing or working various jobs on the boardwalk. After we graduated from Ocean City High, Joe went off to the University of Delaware and I headed to Lafayette, but we rendezvoused each summer, falling back into our comfortable rituals; surfing, lying on the beach, water skiing, playing tennis, working nights on the boardwalk, partying, trying to pick up girls, and arguing over who was better at everything.

Living in a privileged, comfortable cocoon, we remained sheltered from the forces shaping America. For us, the Civil Rights Movement, race riots and the Vietnam War were all stuff on TV. Sure, we grew our hair long, wore our tie-dyed t-shirts and bell bottoms, griped about the "the Man" and "the Machine" and sported our "Dump Nixon" buttons; but we weren't really affected by larger events. And when it finally looked like the war might rudely insert itself into our lives, we both drew high draft lottery numbers, enabling us to bypass Vietnam completely and go straight to grad school.

Captured by the allure of becoming Tar Heels, we reunited in Chapel Hill, where I enrolled in a master's program in Communications, focusing on Radio and TV Broadcasting, and Joe began working on a degree in Recreation Administration, zeroing in on the concentration God seemingly created with him in mind - Leisure Studies. After rooming together during our first year in Carlson, UNC's only high-rise, graduate dorm, we both scored jobs as resident advisers (RA's), securing free single rooms and modest stipends. By February of our second year, we found ourselves staring at the impending May graduation, just beginning our job searches and wondering how the time had flown by so quickly.

Remaining true to his life's mission, Joe sought a post at a seaside resort. He intended, once again, to spend his mornings surfing; work afternoons overseeing the play of the idle rich; follow dinner with private tennis lessons for beautiful young women; and cruise the evening's array of parties.

I, on the other hand, merely wanted to establish a foothold at a radio station, any radio station, in order to begin living my dream of transforming the AM dial through round-the-clock sports programming. I knew that, after decades of repetition, the top-forty format was stale and that the more recent "all-news-all-the-time" stations were hopelessly boring after one 20-

minute rundown of the day's top stories. Sensing the time was right for something new, I obsessed over the sports niche waiting to be filled. I dreamed of stringing together broadcasts of college and pro games, supplemented by heavy doses of score updates and interviews. First, I'd go local, and later I'd find a way to get the whole package syndicated. I had this "can't miss" vision, needing only an owner and a station manager willing to take a risk.

But our life ambitions weren't on our minds that day in February as we got out of my car and made our way toward the Carlson entrance. Along with about 10 other grad students standing on the front side of the wing-shaped, brick dorm, we stared at the nearly-nude, hulking figure on the fourth floor. Meanwhile, Bikini Guy and his attractive companion were oblivious to the leering crowd below. Peering out at the horizon, he gestured gracefully with one hand, bellowing in badly broken English, seemingly reciting something committed to memory. All the time, she gazed intently at his over-sized head, hanging on his every word.

As we passed beneath the couple, Joe, connoisseur of all things female, commented on the woman's firm figure and attractive face. He also tried to convince me that she was probably growing bored with her companion. Recognizing her physical attributes, but having no idea where Joe was coming up with his other insights, I noticed that Bikini Guy seemed more energetic the closer we drew. "The man's fired up. He's a furnace with energy to burn," I said to Joe.

"Well, he's protected by plenty of insulation," Joe replied. "He probably weighs about two-sixty or more. He's got a pretty high blubber factor. You know, I think I've seen this guy before. Isn't he one of those crazies who takes his shirt off at Packer games; you know, Lambeau Field, ten degrees, a big green "G" painted on his chest?"

"Could be, but he looks more like a Steeler's fan to me, someone who came crawling out of some remote corner of Western Pennsyltucky."

"Plausible," Joe responded, "Whatever he is, he's an exotic species. Let's investigate."

Entering the dorm, we proceeded across its spacious lobby, comfortably furnished with a worn Persian rug, oversized chairs and a sofa, to the information desk window, located next to the Residence Director's office. Suzy, one of our fellow RA's was staffing the desk, her 4'10" frame barely enabling her to look out over the counter.

"So, Suzy, My Dear. Who's the exhibitionist up on my floor?"

"Quite the item, isn't he," Suzy shot back in her thick Long Island accent.

"Yeah, one of a kind. But who is he?"

"He's your new resident."

"OK, but where did he come from?"

"The Soviet Union. He's the famous Vladimir Borzov, but he likes to be called Vladi."

"Vladimir who?"

"Vladimir Borzov, the dissident Russian poet who defected to the U.S. about two weeks ago. Don't you pay attention to anything but the latest sportscast?"

Suzy had a habit of speaking condescendingly regarding my preoccupation with sports. I usually let it roll off of my back, but that day I wasn't in the mood to take it.

"Hey, listen, we can't all get pedigrees in political science, like you. I focus my scholarly attention on what's occurring in the increasingly important dominion of athletics. My future is in sports, and I'm all over what's happening in my corner of the world. I count on colleagues like you to keep me abreast of pertinent international and domestic events. So, please brief me,

Little One. But first, do you want to hear about the Phillies' spring training roster? What about a preview of the ACC basketball tournament? Maybe the upcoming NFL draft? Or can I interest you in the latest men's and women's tennis rankings?"

Glaring at me like I was an absolute moron, Suzy shot back., "Spare me the details, Mister Well-Rounded, but I'll fill you in. Where to start? Maybe I should back up a bit. First, have you heard that there is a war going on?" She asked, uncomfortably upping the ante.

"Ouch! Go easy, Suzy," I responded, defensively. "Yeah, I know there's a war going on. It's not my fault that Nixon's brain trust dreamed up the draft lottery; and that suddenly, like two-thirds of the rest of the guys in America, I'm off the hook. But you know, eventually this war is going to end, and things will be ok again; and you know what will help start making them ok?"

"What?"

"Sports. We'll be playing basketball, soccer, table tennis and other sports against Vietnam and China. It will be sports that'll help us get us get connected again. So let's not go knocking sports and the people who like them just because they're not intellectually fashionable. Okay?"

Managing to back off, while getting in one last shot, Suzy retorted, " I apologize for going for your jugular. It's just that you're such an easy target. Let me start over. Vladimir Borzov, noted Russian poet and frequent critic of the single-party Soviet system, was allowed by the Soviet government to make a limited tour of the U.S. in conjunction with the softening of U.S.-Soviet relations prompted by Kissinger's emerging detente policy. While in Washington D.C. last week, Mr. Borzov somehow managed to slip away from the Soviet security detail assigned to watch him, apparently squeezing his sizable body out a bathroom window. He soon showed up at the State Department and requested political asylum. Kissinger allegedly balked, viewing the affair as a threat to his efforts to wedge the U.S. between the Soviets and the Chinese. But our own North Carolina Senator Jesse Helms came to Borzov's rescue. With the election coming up in the fall, Nixon decided that he couldn't handle pressure from the Republican right wing, so the administration caved. The next thing you know, voila! Vladimir Borzov is a Tar Heal with a special teaching fellowship in the UNC Comparative Literature Department."

"Just like I figured, "interjected Joe. "But who is the lovely lady at his side?"

"She's Janine Ashcroft, newly minted Slavic Languages Ph.D., his interpreter and now his apparent roommate. She enrolled in a post-doctoral fellowship and checked into a female double on the third floor. But since Vladi got a single, they've already taken apart the bunk in his room and put the beds next to each other. According to their neighbors, she seems to be already engaging in aerobic workouts with the Russian bear."

"All in the name of improving international relations," inserted Joe.

"Probably out of her deep sympathy and affection for the Soviet people," Suzy responded.

"Things have been calm all year," I chimed in. "I guess we were due for a little excitement. But I really wish that it had been on someone else's floor. I don't need any distractions as I'm headed down to the finish line. But he's here now, so I guess that I'd better get upstairs and introduce myself to the latest addition to Carlson's cast of characters."

* * * * * *

And what a cast of characters we had, with many of them on the Residence Life staff. There was of course Joe with his not quite, dead-on Johnny Cash and Elvis impersonations and his long list of exotic girlfriends. In his year and a half at Carlson he had already dated a fortune teller, a tattoo artist and "Serena" the belly dancer at a Middle Eastern night club in Durham.

Then there was Tony Castelli. A chick-magnet, Sociology doctoral student who'd gotten his master's at SUNY Potsdam; Tony looked like young Billy Joel, but with twice the hair. He cruised around Chapel Hill in the 1964 Buick Electra convertible that he fondly called his "Mercedes."

And there was "Wolf", the bearded, Computer Science Ph. D. candidate who had wandered down from the mountains of North Carolina and had lived in Carlson for thirteen years. Also known as Wolfie, Wolfman and Wolfowitz, he was originally a budding mathematician, but he changed programs when he was close to graduation in order to avoid having to move out of Carlson. Closing in on the time limit for his second program, Wolf was again searching for an academic option in order to prolong his stay in what had long ago become his lair.

"Reverend Al", Carlson's Residence Director and a recent Comparative Religion Ph.D., resembled football player Merlin Olsen, had a penchant for keg parties, and regularly proclaimed the medicinal and spiritual benefits of marijuana. He referred to his twelve RA's as "the Disciples." And he called his Assistant Residence Director, Jonathan - a 6'3", African-American, MBA student and Michigan ROTC graduate - "Jack the Baptist."

In addition to Suzy, the women RA's included Nevada Doris; a law student who had spent three years in Vegas dealing blackjack. Doris ran an ongoing poker game in her room, organized Carlson's annual Casino Night, and preferred her Rolling Rock beer in pony bottles.

Lisa, a.k.a. "Lovely Lisa", was a social work student, resembling and sounding like a young Eartha Kit. Lisa always sang at Carlson's monthly talent shows; and her two, former boyfriends, both of whom were barred by restraining orders, repeatedly tried to crash the shows.

There was also Maxine, a shapely, thirty-five year old medical student who returned to university life after serving as a nurse in a Vietnam M.A.S.H. unit. An adrenaline junkie, Maxine displayed no fear and regularly organized outdoor activities such as hang gliding, rock climbing, and 100-mile bicycle trips for whatever staff or residents she could coerce into joining her.

The four remaining RA's , by contrast, were all pretty tame. Ricardo, a chemistry grad student from Chicago, was unflappable, someone you could always count on in a pinch. Charlotte, my co-RA on the fourth floor, was a calm, steady linguistics student with a B.A. from William and Mary. Unfortunately for her, Charlotte hailed from Charlotte, North Carolina, the source of endless jokes about her parents' lack of imagination. Finally, Scott and Hilary were junior undergrads assigned to the male and female wings of Carlson's only undergraduate floor. Although Reverend Al tapped them to work at Carlson because of their relative maturity, the rest of the staff referred to them as "the Kids."

* * * * * *

"Hey, I'll go up with you," Joe offered as I strode across the lobby toward the elevator. "I don't want to miss the opportunity to meet our very own, Soviet celebrity. Maybe I can help you to communicate with this Russian."

"Yeah, right. Nearly two years in Chapel Hill and you haven't even learned how to speak Southern,"

"OK, Big Guy. I'll not only speak Russian, I'll speak Southern Russian: 'Vodka, Ya'll'?"

"I'm so impressed. Let's go."

As we entered the elevator,   we encountered the exiting Wilma.   A mildly obese, thirtyish law student from Raleigh, Wilma was president of Carlson's Student Association and a resident on my floor. Our conversation didn't do anything to dispel her reputation for lechery.

"Are you headed upstairs to meet the big fella?" Wilma asked.   But before getting an answer she added, "I'd sure like some of that stuff, Darlin'. Would I like some of that! It doesn't get much better. Where was he for the last three years?"

"It looks like he's already taken, Wilma," I suggested.

"I can wait. My time will come, Darlin' "

"Have you met him yet? " Joe asked.

"You can't not meet him, Honey. He's parked himself out there on the deck, practically buck naked, for the last hour and a half. You can't leave your room without running into him. And he talks to everyone. He doesn't seem to speak too much English other than 'Howdy Buddy', but that doesn't stop him. He starts spoutin' words in Russian and that plaything of his tries translating, but she can't keep up. Must be kind of tiring, especially after all the bangin' they've already been doin' in the room."

"Sounds like we need her. Let's hope she stays close by so we can keep the international communications channels open," I offered.

"Not if I can help it, Baby. Not if I can help it," Wilma said, while strolling away. "I'm getting' me some of that stuff."

As the elevator doors were closing, I caught a glimpse of an elderly man dressed in a charcoal grey suit slowly walking across the lobby towards the information desk. Since I'd never seen him before, I made a mental note of yet another stranger appearing at the dorm.

A few moments later, Joe and I were on the fourth floor heading for the balcony that served as an exterior hallway to the floor's multiple, four-room suites. We stepped out onto the concrete walkway and approached Vladi and Janine. I extended my hand and introduced myself.

"Welcome to UNC, Vladi. I'm Eckhardt Larsen, your RA and this is Joe O'Malley one of our third floor RA's"

"Howdy," Vladi responded in his thick accent; firmly grasping my hand, then enthusiastically uttering several sentences in Russian.

Janine introduced herself, shaking hands with Joe then me. She explained that Vladi was expressing his deep gratitude at joining the university and staying at Carslon, although he expected to be moving out at the end of the semester, once he located a suitable apartment.

Suddenly, Vladi grabbed me in a smothering hug, exclaiming "Buddy, friend, yes!"

Shocked by Vladi's impulsive embrace, his strength and his scent, I tried to disengage as quickly as possible. Hoping that a quick affirmation might cause Vladi to turn his attention elsewhere, I heartily agreed, "Yes, Buddy. Good Buddy."

The plan worked and soon Joe was the one with the large paws wrapped around him. "Buddy," Vladi repeated. "God bless USA."

"Vladivostok," exclaimed Joe.

"Vladivostok?," repeated Vladi with a quizzical look. Then with a huge smile on his face, he placed a slobbery kiss on Joe's cheek and began repeating, "Vladivostok! Vladivostok!"

"What did I do?" Joe anxiously asked Janine as Vladi continued hugging him.

"Although Vladi has lived most of his life in Moscow, he was born in Vladivostok. He's deeply touched that you acknowledged this. How did you know?"

"I guess I just sensed it," Joe responded, looking visibly relieved as Vladi released him. "You know, you can take Vladi out of Vladivostok, but you can't take the Vladivostok out of Vladi. Actually, other than vodka, sputnik, and Moscow, Vladivostok is one of the few Russian words I know. But I thought that it meant, 'Hello.'"

"Well, you were wrong, but you may have made a friend for life," Janine laughed. "When Vladi takes to someone, he remains very committed."

"That's great," I chimed in, "I've been looking for someone to share Joe with. And just remember, if you need anything, feel free to call, or knock on my door. I'm just two suites down . Don't hesitate."

"As we waved farewell while sliding by Vladi and Janine, the Russian suddenly boomed, "до свидания, Buddies!". We looked at Janine, quizzically.

"Vladi is saying goodbye. Your knowledge of Russian is now greatly increased. You not only know that 'Vladivostok' doesn't mean 'hello.' You also know that 'до свидания' means 'goodbye.' If you'd like any further lessons, I'll be happy to assist," she added smiling coquettishly.

"I may have to take you up on that," blurted Joe. "Who knows? A trip to the Soviet Union might just be in my future. It's best to be prepared."

Janine flashed another quick smile. As Joe and I turned into my suite, Joe whispered, "She digs me. I can tell."

"Right!" I shot back, sarcastically, as I opened my door and we entered the room. "She was hanging all over him the entire time, except when he was hugging you and me."

"Yeah, but we connected. There's chemistry there. He may be world famous and sound charming in Russian, but he's way overweight and getting older by the minute. He's probably had a thousand women. She knows that. He's not a good long-term investment. I, on the other hand, am young, virile, capable of vastly improving her tennis game, and anxious to be introduced to the beauty of the Russian language."

"She's probably five years older than you."

"That's nothing between soul mates."

"You picked up all of this from her smile?"

"You bet. I've got the sixth sense."

"Well, from what I saw, it looks like Vladi is more attracted to you than Janine . Based on that kiss, you may be taking him home to meet your parents. You 're a cute couple. I'll be upset if I'm not your best man."

"You'll see, Big Guy. This is no joke. This is destiny."

Chapter 2
Olivia

As I mentioned before, my own love life had radically improved the previous fall when I started dating Olivia Russell. At the time, she was a second-year teacher at Hillsborough Friends Academy, a small, Quaker, private school located in the county seat about twelve miles north of Chapel Hill. We met on a Friday night when I interviewed Olivia following the regional, girls' soccer championship game. She was coaching the HFA squad. I was covering the game for WTHL - "Tar Heel:1520 on your AM dial" - the local radio station, where I interned.

Even before the Federal Title IX legislation mandated full equity for girls sports, North Carolina was an emerging hotbed of girls' soccer. Olivia was the founding coach of the Hillsborough Friends girls' team, and was receiving substantial press coverage for developing a high caliber team in only her second year on the job. Olivia was bright, pretty, energetic and competitive as hell, all appealing traits to me. She was also coming off of a relationship gone sour with the HFA basketball coach, Hank Stoddard. Although considered "a hunk" by many local women, Stoddard's chauvinism wore on Olivia, who dumped him after a few months.

The HFA Conductors – a nickname drawn from North Carolina Quakers' involvement in the Underground Railroad - lost the tightly contested championship on corner kicks to Raven's Nest, the state's elite girls' program. I was the last of the local reporters to talk to Olivia following the game. Feeling badly about having stuck yet another microphone in her face following a heartbreaking loss, after the few obligatory quotes, I quickly turned off the tape recorder and complimented Olivia on her team's hard-fought effort.

"Your girls played great, Coach."

"Thanks. Tough one to lose though. They're taking it hard."

"It's got to be especially rough on the seniors."

"Yeah, fortunately we only have three. With so many kids coming back next year, we should be in pretty good shape."

"I was watching you talk to them after the game. You've got a strong sense of family within the team. It carries over onto the field. They're really conscious of each other, very unselfish. I liked their passing, always willing to give the ball up, rather than forcing shots. And they were constantly encouraging each other."

"You noticed all that, huh? That's real important to me. My high school coach stressed it a lot."

"Where'd you play?"

"North Plainfield, New Jersey. But I didn't really play. My high school didn't have a girls' team. I was a manager for the guys, but Coach Chyzowych saw that I had some talent and that I loved the game. We didn't have enough boys to field two teams, so he let me scrimmage at all of the practices."

"You worked with Walt Chyzowych?"

"Yeah, you've heard of him?"

"Of course, he's a legend in American soccer."

"Yeah, but I didn't expect to run into somebody down

here who knows about him. How'd you   learn about Chyzowych?"

"I'm something of a sports freak and I'm from Jersey, too, Ocean City. He starred for the Philadelphia Tryzub Ukrainian Nationals and was an All-American at Temple in the sixties. I think that he played on the U.S. team back around '65."

"My God, you do know about him. Do you play?"

"No. I mean, I can play, but I never played on a school team. I play co-ed, rec-league soccer in Chapel Hill. You know, "Rainbow Soccer."

"Of course I know Rainbow Soccer. Everybody living anywhere near here knows about Rainbow Soccer. I play Rainbow Soccer, too; but I don't remember seeing you."

"Maybe that's because my soccer playing isn't all that noticeable. I'm a distance runner. I ran in high school and college. But I know a lot about soccer and other sports. To tell the truth, I probably know too much about sports."

"Well, it's cool that you noticed what a tight group our team is and that you know about Chyzowych. It's really cool. Listen, I've got to go. I'm taking the team to Papa Joe's in Hillsborough for Pizza. Do you want to come along?"

"Sounds great. Let me call in my story, and I'll meet you there."

"Alright. But, I'm sorry, I wasn't paying attention when we started talking, what'd you say your name is again?"

"Larsen. Eckhardt Larsen."

"Eckhardt Larsen. That's unusual."

"That's because it's two last names. Eckhardt was my grandmother's maiden name. I've gone through life without a real first name. It's the cross that I bear, but it does make me sort of distinctive. Even when people shorten it to 'Eck,' there's never any confusion about who they're talking to. I'm always the only Eckhardt or Eck in any crowd."

"Hmmm. Eck sounds short for 'heck' or 'wreck' or 'yeck.' It doesn't work for me. You look more like a 'Larsen' to me. Does anyone call you 'Larsen?'

"Well there was a bully in seventh grade, but I've gotten over it."

"Good, cause I like it and I'm going to call you 'Larsen.' I'll see you at Papa Joe's in twenty minutes, Larsen"

It happened that quickly, that unexpectedly. Pretty much from the moment we met, we managed to find ways to talk or see each other every day; and we stayed together, never having any serious fights or any real doubts. We enjoyed each other's company and supported each other's efforts. I listened to Olivia's coaching strategies and her problems with her English classes, offering a suggestion here or there, but mostly just listening while Olivia worked things out for herself. And Olivia critiqued the taped reports that I prepared for WTHL, or the articles that I was writing for *The Daily Tar Heel*, the campus newspaper. And, for good measure, we got ourselves assigned to the same Rainbow Soccer team.

An added perk was that Olivia owned her own house in Hillsborough; a small, three-bedroom, brick bungalow with a front porch, large enough for a few rocking chairs. It was on a corner lot about a half mile from the center of the historic downtown. A huge oak in the side yard loomed over the house, providing comforting shade during the hot, Carolina summer and allowing Olivia to forsake air conditioning in favor of ceiling fans. A small drainage ditch, lined with day lilies angled through the property. On the inside, Olivia decorated sparsely, but tastefully, favoring futons along with the batiks and oriental wall hangings that she began collecting while a student at Guilford College in Greensboro.

From the time that Olivia and I realized that we had become "a couple", about a month after we met, I spent as much of my free time as possible at her house; but free time was rare for both of us. My RA position demanded that I spend weeknights at the dorm, and once a month I drew weekend duty. Also, on top of my four graduate classes, I had to put in ten internship hours a week at WTHL. Meanwhile, Olivia's teaching, committee work, and coaching - lacrosse in the spring in addition to soccer in the fall - kept her incredibly busy. Neither of us had time to sit around missing the other, and we learned to make the most of the time that we did have together. I spent every weekend that I wasn't on duty at Olivia's; but although Olivia would visit the dorm for parties, she drew the line at spending nights at the dorm, in spite of my pleas that she join me.

"When we get married, we can be together all the time," Olivia stated flatly. "It's better this way. We both get one weekend a month where we can use the time to get our work done. We don't have to sleep in a cramped, single bed, and I don't have to use that dirty suite bathroom. Plus, you know that I can't really get a good night's sleep with all of the noise at Carlson. I'm too old for dorm life."

"You're only twenty-four."

"Yeah, but since I started teaching tenth graders every day, I've aged. Believe me. If you haven't taught high school you don't know how draining it is."

"That's why you have to come over and take a bigger sip of college life. You'll rediscover your coed within. And I'm just the guy to help you do it," I parried, knowing that I was getting nowhere.

"Right, spare me the favor. We'll be better off once you're out of the dorm."

She brushed awkwardly close to the issue of what I would be doing after graduation, a topic we generally avoided because of the slim probability of me getting a job at a radio station or a newspaper in the area. It was an especially sensitive matter because Olivia loved her job, and didn't want to leave HFA. So, we chose not to talk about it, hoping that somehow things would work out in the end. Fortunately, for anyone wishing to practice denial during the winter months in the Raleigh–Durham-Chapel Hill area, basketball provides the perfect diversion.

In case you happen to be from another planet, basketball is the great obsession in North Carolina, and a steady stream of games provided Olivia and me a convenient opportunity to combine work with pleasure. The radio station assigned its two full-time sports reporters to the UNC, Duke and N.C. State games. Their half-time reporter covered Chapel Hill High School and Orange High (the county high school); while I – the lowly intern - was assigned the HFA boys and girls varsity basketball games. Olivia didn't coach in the winter, but she was expected to attend most basketball games in order to support the teams and to monitor student behavior. Since the HFA home games were held on Wednesday afternoons and Friday evenings, Olivia and I typically ate supper together after Wednesday games and before Friday contests, and we traveled together in my car to away games. The arrangement was ideal, except for the problem of spending so much game time in close proximity to Hank Stoddard, the coach Olivia had dumped.

Although Olivia had no further interest in him, Stoddard, figuring that it was only a matter of time until she grew tired of me, was convinced that Olivia would soon want to get back together with him. Making matters worse, before and after every game I had to interview Stoddard. He was always overly ingratiating while the tape recorder was on, and boorish as soon as I switched it off. I so wanted to catch him on tape acting like an asshole, and find a way to get him on the air.

And then there was the coup-de-grace. During games,

Stoddard flashed longing stares at Olivia. She appeared oblivious, but it wore on me; so I mentioned it to her once, fishing for reassurance.

"Relax, Larsen. You're safe. Believe me, the only time Hank ever really looks "longingly" at someone is when he stares in a mirror."

Chapter 3
Jonas

In spite of Hank Stoddard, I was enthralled with HFA's team. For the first time in recent memory, they were exceptionally good, primarily because of a very special player, Lithuanian phenom, Jonas Petraitis.   Among the area's high school basketball fans, Jonas, not Vladi Borzov, was the local "Iron Curtain" celebrity.   Born and raised in basketball-crazed Vilnius, Lithuania –sort of the Carolina of the Baltics - Jonas was the son of legendary Vilnius Boys Club basketball coach, Vytautas Petraitis; a man so obsessed with "the game" that he began putting his only son through hours of dribbling and passing drills at age four. By his early teens, young Jonas was among the most talented Lithuanian players in his age group, and clearly possessed the best work ethic. At fifteen, he came off of the bench as a shooting guard for the 18 and under Lithuanian Junior National Team, receiving substantial playing time due to his sure ball-handling skills and deadly outside marksmanship. By sixteen, following a summer growth spurt during which he reached his full height of six foot four, he was a starter capable of playing either guard or power forward, and of driving hard to the basket. His lean, hard body grew strong from long hours in the weight room; and at seventeen, Jonas emerged as that rare commodity, a tall, dominating point guard.

He became the team's assist leader, while also grabbing 7-8 rebounds per game and settling in as the team's second leading scorer, surpassed only by their dominating seven-foot center, Mantas Kavolis.

Life in Vilnius was good for the promising young player. A mature and quietly engaging fellow, he was doing what he loved, all the time receiving the benefits of a pampered athlete in a communist country; individual tutoring, supplemental clothing and food allowances, the attention of young women and international travel. Then, out of nowhere, tragedy struck. While Jonas was abroad playing in a tournament in Warsaw, his father and his mother, Audronò, were killed in an auto accident.

Jonas received the news in the locker room, immediately after completing the finest, all-around game of his young career; twenty-six points, ten assists and twelve rebounds. Though devastated, he shed few tears. Jonas was, after all, a stoic. His father had insisted on that.

Following the funeral, the young star retreated deeper and deeper into basketball. His previously rigorous approach became scarily obsessive. Hours after practice ended, he remained alone in the gym shooting jump shots and free throws, working on dribbling, and running wind sprints from baseline to baseline. His game continued to improve; but his studies suffered and Jonas showed little interest in socializing with his fellow players or in dating, a marked departure for the handsome, dark-haired teenager.

In late October of 1971, the Lithuanian Junior National Team traveled to Canada for a good will tour against Canadian college teams, who they repeatedly out-classed. After dominating Xavier and Dalhousie in Nova Scotia, the team headed west to Hamilton, Ontario to play McMaster University. Unbeknownst to the Lithuanian coaches and Jonas' teammates,

Hamilton was the home of Jonas' closest living relative; his father's younger sister, Rytò. In 1945, at age twenty, Rytò, with her family's blessing, fled to freedom during the Soviet occupation of Lithuania. With the assistance of the Lithuanian Resistance, Rytò, a remarkably resourceful woman, avoided the Red Army, crossed the Lithuanian border, and made her way across Poland and Soviet-occupied Eastern Germany. Once behind U.S. and British lines, she continued on to Denmark, where she met Stephen O'Henly, a young Canadian Quaker working as a volunteer for the International Red Cross. The two fell in love, married and returned to Canada where Stephen took a job as a mathematics teacher at Woolman Hall, a Quaker boarding school in Hamilton. After 15 year of teaching, Stephen became the Head of the school. Meanwhile, Rytò, pursued a nursing degree at the University of Toronto and later became a physician, completing her M.D. at McMaster and subsequently practicing pediatrics in a small office adjacent to Woolman Hall. She and Stephen lived in a house on the school's grounds with their two teenage children.

The Lithuanian basketball game with McMaster was scheduled for a Saturday night. Following another relatively easy Lithuanian victory, the team hustled off the floor into the visitor's locker room. The head coach, Ivan Tovadis, called his players together for a brief post-game talk, only to discover that Jonas was absent. When Jonas didn't respond to the coach's calls, his teammates fanned out through the locker room and the field house looking for him, but with no luck. Jonas was gone.

Nobody had noticed that the gym bag Jonas placed behind the team's bench before the game contained a full change of clothing. Nor had anyone detected that, as the team headed for the locker room, Jonas stalled so as to be last in line, peeled off down a small corridor under the stands and left the gym via a nearby exit. By the time anyone knew that he was missing, Jonas was seated in a car, driven by Rytò, heading for the seclusion of Woolman Hall.

Legally, Jonas was an orphaned minor still six months shy of his eighteenth birthday. In spite of his alien status, under Canadian law, Rytò, as next of kin, was able to petition for legal guardianship. Since she and Stephen were both well-known and well-connected within Hamilton, the paperwork was processed promptly. Furthermore, the Lithuanian government, always more independent than most Soviet dominated satellites, respected blood relationships and made only a token protest. Thus, Jonas obtained Canadian residency by mid-November, virtually in record time and without a major international incident. But his stay in Hamilton was short, for Jonas was pursuing far more than a quiet life with his Canadian relatives. Even as he and Rytò were fleeing the McMaster campus, Jonas shared his intentions. The words came pouring out in the heavily accented, but fluent English that he had been studying since elementary school.

"Aunt Rytò?"

"Yes, Jonas"

"My father was a fan of North Carolina basketball ever since 1957, when he listened to Radio Free Europe broadcasts of the Tarheel's NCAA tournament semi-final victory over Michigan State and their national championship win over Wilt Chamberlain and the University of Kansas. He loved to tell how Coach Frank McGuire's team took three overtimes to win each of the games and how they never gave up. He especially admired Pete Brennan, the UNC forward. I'll always remember Father describing how, with 11 seconds remaining in the first overtime of the Michigan State game, Brennan grabbed a rebound on a missed Spartan free throw; raced down court; and while double covered, hit a jumper from the foul line to tie the game and force a second overtime. The next year, his senior season, Brennan was a first team All-American and the Atlantic Coast Conference Player of the Year. He was a great one."

Rytò nodded as Jonas raced on.

"Most of my life, I have heard Father's stories about Coach Dean Smith's teams; how, even though they have yet to win a national championship, they are destined to do so because of their great talent, discipline and teamwork. Father told me about "The Kangaroo Kid," Billy Cuningham, and about Bob Lewis, Larry Miller, and Charlie Scott. I know all about the current team with Robert McAdoo, Dennis Wuycik, George Karl, Bill Chamberlain, and Bobby Jones. They will have a great year. They are good enough to win the whole thing."

"Aunt Rytò, it was always Father's dream that I might play for the Tar Heels. It's also my dream. I want to wear the Carolina Blue like Pete Brennan and all the other great Carolina players. I might never be as good as they are, but I must try. I have no time to waste. I must immediately move to the United States to have any chance of being scouted and winning a scholarship."

Having spit out his message, Jonas grew quiet, sat back against the car seat and waited, uncertain of the response he would receive. Most people would have been stunned at such an outburst. But Rytò hadn't lived a normal life. She, too, had chased a dream, making dramatic, split-second decisions impacting the rest of her life. She, too, understood her brother Vytautas' extraordinary passion for basketball and she could tell that the same intensity burned deeply within his son. She may have been the only person in the world who would not try to discourage Jonas. Indeed, she chose to do everything in her power to assist him.

"Jonas, I understand.   Stephen and I will do all that we can to help you. But you are my last link to my family, you must promise to come and visit on your vacations. Ok?"

Visibly relieved, Jonas chuckled his response, "Ok, I promise. Of course, I promise."

* * * * * *

At such a late date, obtaining a scholarship to UNC for the following year was probably hopeless, so Rytò and Stephen explored with Jonas alternative strategies for fulfilling his dream. They suggested that the best way to get noticed by coach Smith would be to appear, virtually in his backyard, playing for a nearby school. They also indicated that by attending a private school, Jonas might be able to play two full seasons of high school basketball, one during his current, senior year and one during a post-graduate season. If, as expected, a scholarship was not available due to UNC's 1972-1973 recruiting class already being filled, there might be a reasonable chance of making the entering class of 1973-1974. And even if the Tarheels chose not to extend him an offer, Jonas might, in two years, establish a reputation meriting scholarships from other Division I schools with highly competitive programs.

North American Quakers are few in number, but they are tightly networked. Stephen knew the heads of the two Quaker schools in close proximity to the University of North Carolina, HFA in Hillsborough and Carolina Friends School, just outside of Durham. Conversations with both indicated to Stephen that HFA would be the better fit for Jonas, as it had the greater athletic ambitions of the two. And since, in addition to being an exceptional athlete, Jonas was a bright, bilingual fellow offering some much needed diversity to HFA , the admissions office immediately admitted him at the beginning of the second trimester. So, incredibly, at the start of December, just as the basketball season was starting, Jonas found himself living with a host family in Hillsborough and attending HFA.

From the moment he landed, gift-wrapped, on Hank Stoddard's doorstep, Jonas excelled, establishing himself quickly in non-conference games and during the Carolina Independent School Conference schedule. Playing where asked to play, rather than stepping in at point guard, he switched between two-guard and forward, racking up occasional triple doubles, while averaging 22 points, 9 rebounds and 8 assists. Meanwhile, HFA built an 18–2 record by Presidents' weekend, the best record in school history. All was going according to plan.

Chapter 4
The Game

On the last Friday in February, Olivia and I met for dinner at Olivia's house before driving to HFA for the boy's basketball game. As we sat talking in the cozy, brightly decorated kitchen, I was especially excited.

"Tonight is really big!"

"Yeah, Durham High is always good. It should be a great game, but its non-conference, and we have the CISC tournament next week. We might have a letdown,"

Olivia responded.

"I don't think so. Jonas is going to be pumped. The word is that Dean Smith is sending his assistant, Freddie Vogle, to scout the game. They have one scholarship left to offer now that Mitch Kupchak has signed his letter of intent, and they've been leaning towards some junior college player out of Kansas; but the guy might want to stay close to home and play in the Big Eight. Jonas has apparently caught Dean's eye. I didn't think that he had a prayer this year, but it just might work out."

"Cool."

"I'll say. Tonight is his chance to show what he's got because the competition is so good. Durham High has only lost one game all season. They've got great speed in the backcourt, and they're big up front; but I think that Jonas and the rest of the team are up to the challenge. On the other hand, Dave

Olson is their coach, and he's probably the best in the state. If anybody can figure out a way to shut us down, it's him."

Olivia was familiar with Olson, a former star athlete and captain of the basketball team at Guilford College, who graduated several years ahead of her. "That man is going to be a major college coach someday," she chimed in. "Just like Hank."

"Oh, low blow. You really know how to hurt a guy. With each game that HFA wins, he becomes more smug after our interviews, and now you're serving him up during dinner. I sure hope that's sarcasm."

"Of course it is, Larsen. I was just teasing. You know that you've won the real prize," she cooed as she approached me, wrapped her arms around my shoulders and gave me a long kiss.

"True," I acknowledged. "Winning basketball games loses out every time to making love with the woman of your dreams."

"Absolutely," she whispered rubbing up closely against me. "But right now we're running late. We've got to get to this particular basketball game so you can tape your pre-game comments with said fat-head, coach and call your report to the station."

"I think we have time, Olivia. It's a home game. If we're fast…"

"Larsen, have you lost your mind?"

"Temptress. How can you toy with me like this?"

" Later, Larsen. Later. Let's go."

"Ok." I answered, trying to calm down. "We're out of here."

* * * * * *

With North Carolina's private and public schools holding separate state championship tournaments, this was the only time during the year that HFA and the Durham Bulldogs would meet. Forty-five minutes before tip-off, the tension and excitement were running high. The stands in HFA's cramped, 500-seat gym were already packed and the fire marshal was on hand to make sure that none of the fifty or so overflow fans mingling outside were allowed in.

As the teams went through their shooting drills, I went through the ritual of obtaining brief, taped statements from both coaches; before adding my own comments and quickly calling in the pre-game report to WTHL. Calm and collected, Coach Olson offered a stark contrast to the anxious, stuttering Hank, who knew he was in way over his head in this coaching match-up.   At best, only an average strategist subject to painfully silly mistakes under pressure; Hank tended to stick with a man-to-man defense long after it was obvious that a switch to a zone was necessary. Or he'd full-court press too long, unnecessarily tiring his players. Sometimes, he'd even lose track of how many fouls his players had committed. Once, early in the second half, he took Jonas out of a game when he only had two fouls, forgot about him, and left him sitting on the bench as a 20-point lead slipped away.

But fate had smiled on Hank this particular year. The other HFA players' skills meshed beautifully with Jonas' exceptional talents, and they were able to bail Hank out of trouble all season long. The Conductors won most games easily, and pulled out all but a few tightly contested matches in spite of their coach.

In addition to Jonas, HFA's starters included the Weitz brothers, Tom a 6'2", senior, small forward and Taylor, the teams 5'll", sophomore, point guard. Second generation German Americans and the sons of two UNC professors, neither of the Weitz boys were Division I college prospects; but both were hard-nosed competitors, well-schooled in the game, who rarely committed mistakes. The team's other forward, alternating with Jonas at two guard when Jonas moved inside, was Howie Jackson, a slender, 6'2", African-American junior with quick moves, a deft shooting touch and serious jumping ability. Finally, there was Charles Graeves at center. Though only 6'3", an inch shorter than Jonas, Charles, an African – American senior, was fast, muscular and, with his 230 lb. body, capable of taking up a lot of space in the lane. Charles controlled the paint, even against substantially taller opponents.

The Conductors' great weakness was their bench. They barely had one. HFA was a small school. The team could only draw upon a pool of 225 students in grades seven through twelve, and sixty percent of these students were girls. Although senior, sixth-man Sam Carrelli was a strong kid with fundamentally sound skills, at 6-foot he was too short for forward and too slow to play guard. But Carrelli was head and shoulders better than the team's remaining four players who only made the varsity because ten members were needed in order to scrimmage during practice. Consequently, the Conductors had to avoid foul trouble like the plague.

At tip-off, it wasn't clear how HFA and Durham would match up against each other. Durham started two, 6-foot, lightning-fast, African-American guards and an agile, 6'6" African American center, flanked by two sturdy 6'3" white forwards. There were no obvious weaknesses among their first five, and they could go three deep on their bench, replacing all but their center, without sacrificing much talent. On paper, the Bulldogs had the edge in speed, height and coaching, but with good young teams you can never tell how things are going to play out. Getting hot or cold early can lead to an apparently insurmountable lead, which can miraculously dissolve down the stretch depending on the foul situation and whether or not either team is hitting its free throws.

As it turned out, the HFA-Durham game featured no such leads. The two teams traded basket-for-basket, steal-for-steal and rebound-for–rebound throughout the entire game. Both coaches stuck with their bread and butter approaches; Olson a two-three zone defense and Hank his man-to-man. And both relied on a half-court defense pretty much throughout the game, throwing in an occasional full-court press trying to trip up the other team, but to no avail. They were like two talented boxers, relentlessly stalking each other, round-after-round. At half-time, Durham was up 37-36, and the lead seesawed back and forth throughout the second half. Then, with three minutes left to go, and the game tied 61-61, Hank called a time-out.

Throughout, Jonas had been at the top of his game, scoring 25 points, grabbing 9 rebounds, and dishing out 5 assists. At point guard, Taylor Weitz had protected the ball, hit 10 points from the outside, and served up a game-high 11 assists. His brother, Tom, while only scoring five, had hit the boards hard and played tenacious defense. In an impressive display of accuracy, Howie Jackson had tossed up 14 points on 5 of 7 shooting, including three powerful dunks, and was four-out-of-four from the charity stripe. Meanwhile, Charles Graeves, the team's final starter, had contributed 7points and 13 rebounds, while holding Durham's towering center to a mere 8 points and 6 rebounds. But Charles had drawn four fouls in the process, and was perilously close to fouling out of the game. Sam, the only player to come off of the HFA bench, hadn't scored; but had dutifully given others a breather, while playing tight defense on whatever players he was assigned. However, he too had drawn four fouls.

Other than Charles and Sam, no HFA's players were in foul trouble; but Durham, with its talented bench, had nobody with more than two fouls. With the game coming down to the wire, the Conductors' lack of depth had been exposed. Durham could play aggressively knowing Charles was going to have to sit back, close to the basket, to keep from fouling out. The Bulldog's would go hard to the hoop, looking for contact; knowing that, even if called for charging, they had several fouls to spare. During the time-out, Hank, sweating profusely, pleaded with his team to slow down the pace, work their standard offense and look for the good shot. He also decided, in an effort to protect Charles from drawing his final foul, to move him to forward, while sliding Howie into the pivot.

Olivia and I were sitting three rows up in the stands directly behind the HFA bench. While Hank spoke to the team, I scanned the bleachers, quickly spotting Vladi and Janine sitting arm-in-arm about ten rows up in the bleachers at mid-court on the HFA side. I had told them about the game and was pleased to see that they had turned out to support Vladi's fellow émigré, Jonas. Freddie Vogle, the Carolina assistant coach, hadn't been at courtside during the first half of the game, but he arrived early in the second half and was standing at one of the entrances to the gym near the baseline. Knowing that the gym was filled to capacity and that many people had been turned away, I chuckled thinking that here in "Blue Heaven" a fire marshal wouldn't think twice about looking the other way so a UNC coach could see a game.

Then, while glancing back toward center court, I spotted a vaguely familiar figure seated in the first row on the opposite side of the gym; an older guy, gray-haired, solidly built, ramrod straight; dressed in a charcoal grey suit, white shirt and black tie. I couldn't place him at first; but as play resumed, it hit me.

"That's the old guy who was hanging around the Carlson lobby the day Vladi showed up," I thought. "I wonder what he's doing here?"

There wasn't time to consider the question further as, at that precise moment, one of Durham's guards stole the HFA inbound pass, raced down the court and laid the ball in; just as Jonas, who hadn't been near the inbounds play, caught up from behind, barely missing an acrobatic block. The Conductor's were now down by two with two minutes and fifty-five seconds left on the clock. The Durham fans went wild.

Jonas took the ball from the referee and in-bounded it to Taylor, who calmly walked it up court. Suddenly, Hank jumped up from the bench and signaled to Taylor to call another timeout. Looking startled, the young guard complied.

"Jesus!" I shouted to Olivia. "Why in the hell is he doing that? He's out of time-outs, and there are still nearly three minutes left in the game. What a bonehead move!"

My eyes shifted to UNC's Freddie Vogle, shaking his head in disbelief at Hank squandering the precious time-out. He was probably also asking himself why Hank would want to risk another inbounds pass at mid-court when Durham would use the time-out to set up a defense to deny the Conductors the ball?

From where Olivia and I sat, we couldn't hear exactly what Hank was telling the team, but from his frantic gestures it looked like he wanted the ball to go inside. I assumed that either Jonas or Taylor would drive the center lane, look for the open shot, or dish off to Howie or Charles. No matter who ended up taking the shot, there was always a good chance of drawing a foul in heavy traffic around the basket. If the shot went in and there was a foul, HFA might get a three-point play.

Sure enough, Hank had Tom Weitz inbound the ball to Taylor, who, in spite of tight coverage, made a clean catch and quickly dribbled to the top of the key. When it was apparent that he didn't have a clear lane to the basket, Taylor passed the ball back to a trailing Jonas, who had managed to get a step on his defender. Jonas slashed towards the basket. The tall, agile Durham center switched off of Charles in an attempt to block

Jonas' shot. With Jonas in mid-air attempting a finger roll directly in front of the basket, the center, coming from the side in order to avoid body contact, poised his outreached hand to swipe the ball away. But somehow, Jonas pulled the ball back, leaving the center swatting thin air. And as the Durham player's hand flew by his ear, Jonas dropped a soft pass to Charles who elevated for an easy lay-up.

The HFA fans exploded. With two minutes and forty-seven seconds left, the score was once again tied; and Hank wasn't looking so dumb after all. Then, Durham in-bounded the ball and pushed it quickly up court. Their point guard drove the lane. Charles slid in front of him hoping to draw an offensive foul. In fact, his feet were securely planted before the HFA player arrived. It should have been an offensive foul, but Charles didn't get the call. Instead, the referee blew his whistle and indicated that Charles was guilty of a blocking foul. With 2:40 remaining, he fouled out of the game.

Having no timeouts remaining, HFA was in deep trouble. While the Durham guard stepped to the line to sink the first of his two free throws, Hank was forced to send in Sam Carrelli to play two guard, moving Jonas to forward. But, because he had no time outs remaining, Hank couldn't talk to his team, other than shouting commands from the sideline, or briefly conversing with Taylor during either team's free throws. Only if Durham called a time out would there be any remaining opportunity for the coach to carefully dictate strategy. The players were pretty much on their own.

"Come to think of it, this may not be so bad," I thought to myself, as the Durham guard sank his second foul shot, again putting HFA down by two. "The guys are smart. They've got good instincts. They all know that Sam won't be touching the ball. This may keep Hank from fouling things up."

Over the next two and one half minutes, the four

remaining HFA starters rose to the occasion, cranking their offense up a notch; and at Jonas' command, switching to an aggressive half-court, zone defense. Sam avoided errors, even managing to come up with two HFA possessions by diving after loose balls. But the Durham players also elevated the level of their play, and the game became a furious exchange of precision passes, fiercely contested rebounds and beautifully executed shots. Tom Weitz, in particular, stepped up for HFA, collecting four boards and six points by converting three baseline drives. Howie and Jonas each picked up a basket, while playing smothering defense against Durham's front line. However, the two Bulldog guards were shooting the lights out, converting jump shots launched deep from the outside. Throughout, both teams' fans went berserk.

A little more than two minutes was played with neither a foul, nor a timeout. Then, with twenty seconds remaining, and still clinging to a two-point lead, Coach Olson had one of his guards signal time-out to the referee. Anticipating a foul from the Conductors, who had to get the ball even if it meant risking Durham sinking free throws, Olson gathered his team around him for instructions. Simultaneously, Hank knelt in the center of HFA barking his commands. I assumed that Olson was telling his players that they should keep the ball in the hands of their best free throw shooters; while doing their best to avoid any close contact with HFA players, until there was so little time on the clock that even a missed front end of a one-and-one free throw would not give HFA time to get down the court, score and send the game into overtime. I also figured that Hank was telling his guys to prevent any interior penetration by Durham, while maintaining a tight, zone-press defense; hoping for the clean steal, but fouling if the clock got down as low as ten seconds.

When play resumed events unfurled as I suspected, except

for one thing. As the clock wound down to ten seconds, the ball was in Sam's zone; and he forgot to foul the Durham guard that he was defending. Recognizing what had happened Taylor abandoned his zone to help out, quickly hacking the Bulldog player. Still, precious time had been lost. Only six seconds remained.

The Durham guard stepped to the free throw line for the front end of the one-and-one. With three-point baskets still over a decade away from being incorporated into the high school game, making the shot would virtually seal the win for the Bulldogs. Standing on the foul line, the guard dribbled the ball three times, drew a deep breath, raised the ball above his head and launched his shot. From where I was sitting, the shot had a sweet-looking arc, but it grazed the back of the basket, catching just enough iron to bounce to the front rim, where it hung for an agonizing second before rolling out of the cylinder. In a flash, Jonas leaping from his position on the edge of the foul lane, grabbed the ball as it came off the hoop. Without hesitating to look for the outlet pass, he stormed down court, blowing by the Durham shooter and the two front-court players who had been stationed for the rebound.

Crossing mid-court with a mere three seconds remaining, he was picked up by the two Durham defenders who had stayed back on defense. As the two backpedaled providing resistance designed to prevent a clean shot while avoiding a foul, Jonas crossed the ball from his right hand to his left, accelerated, and miraculously split the tiny seam between the two Durham players. Halfway between mid-court and the top of the key, Jonas elevated, shifted the ball back to his right hand, and launched an arching shot. As the ball was leaving Jonas' hand, one of the two Durham players beaten on defense, desperately made a swipe from the rear. Though achingly close to getting a clean block, he missed his target, flailing only thin air. Then, off balance and unable to control his momentum, he collided with Jonas. The two landed in a heap while the ball swished through the net as the time on the clock expired. The referee closest to the play signaled the shot was good; then, with dramatic flair, charged the Durham player with a foul. Pandemonium broke loose in the gym.

"Holy shit!" I thought, as I stood cheering. "What a play. What a big-time, big-league play!"

The Durham player didn't protest. He had made a split-second decision, taken a risk, and screwed up. He knew that he had committed the foul. Dejected, he rose from the floor, glanced at his coach, saw no signs of anger or disappointment; then moved toward his designated position behind the foul shooter. Jonas, meanwhile, stood and headed towards the foul line. On his first step, he winced noticeably, and reached down, grabbing his right knee. A hush fell over the fans.

"Oh, God! He's hurt," Olivia cried; speaking for everyone, even the Durham supporters, in the Gym.

Jonas gingerly limped two or three steps, flexed his knee a few times, then straightened up and moved to the line. As the referee handed him the ball, he asked Jonas something. Jonas shook his head in a manner indicating that he was ok, and bounced the ball a few times in front of him. The HFA fans remained silent. The Durham fans began yelling wildly, hoping to distract the Lithuanian assassin who had just stuck a dagger in their team's heart. Their efforts were to no avail. Jonas, wasting no time, coolly sank the free throw. HFA won one of the best high school games to ever grace a Carolina gym.

The Conductors celebrated wildly in the middle of the court, while the solemn Bulldogs gathered around their coach. The two teams lined up and passed each other, slapping hands and saying the obligatory "good game". As they did, the HFA fans milled about in the stands, laughing and smiling, unwilling to let go of the moment.

Olivia and I hugged immediately following Jonas' winning shot, and quickly made plans to meet in the gym lobby in half-an-hour, after I finished my post-game interviews. Then, I headed over to the Durham bench, to collect a few quotes for my report.

"Coach," I called out, microphone extended, as I approached Dave Olson. "Can you share a few thoughts on the game?"

"Well, that final six seconds about says it all. Both teams played great. It was a fantastic game, and we got beat on a remarkable play by one of the finest athletes we're ever likely to compete against."

"Any regrets?" I blurted, immediately wishing that I could retract the stupid question.

Olson flashed me a brief "Well, what in the hell do you think?" look; but gave a straight answer.

"Not with the way my guys played. I wish that our last free throw had fallen. We could have let them run up the floor uncontested for a lay-up, and we would have still won. But it just wasn't in the cards tonight."

"I guess not, but good luck with the rest of the season coach. I wish you the best." I meant it. Olson was a class act, and Durham was a strong bet for the public school state championship. I hoped that the Bulldogs would go all the way.

We shook hands and Olson headed towards the visitors' locker room. I made a bee-line towards Hank Stoddard, still standing in front of the HFA bench along with Jonas, Freddie Vogle, and the now seemingly, ever-present old gent in the black suit. The old fellow appeared to be dominating the discussion, as though holding court with the younger men. But as I came near, he bid the group farewell and headed toward the nearest exit.

"Who is that guy?" I murmured to myself. But I was quickly distracted from any further thoughts about him as I overheard the conversation developing among Vogle, Stoddard and Jonas.

"Congratulations, Coach," the fast-talking, New York born and bred Vogle said, extending his hand to Hank. "You must be feelin' pretty good."

"You bet, Freddie." Hank responded giddily. "We were saved by one of those Lithuanian lay-ups." Laughing heartily at his own joke.

Turning to Jonas, Vogle again extended his hand. "That was a great all-around game and a tremendous finishing shot, Jonas."

"Like Pete Brennan?" Jonas asked, smiling.

"Now that you mention it, quite a bit like Pete Brennan; but from the film I've seen of that game, you launched yours from farther out. How'd you know about Pete Brennan?"

"My father was the biggest Tar Heel fan in Vilnius," Jonas responded. "I grew up hearing about Coach McGuire and the championship season."

"A Lithuanian Tar Heel. How about that! By the way, Coach Smith sends his regards. He'd hoped to come out to watch tonight's game, but he had a long-standing speaking engagement that he couldn't break. He also asked me to tell you, that if you'd like to make an official recruiting trip to campus, we'd like to extend an invitation to you. We've already offered our full quota of scholarships for next year. But your coach has told me that you might be enrolling for a year of post-grad study here at HFA. If so, we're very interested in talking to you about the year after next. You've convinced me that you can make the step up to Atlantic Coast Conference competition. Realistically, it is probably in your best interest to spend another year adjusting to living in the U.S. It's smart to get your academics squared away. Your English is good, but there's a vast difference between the whole high school scene, and tackling college courses, while playing a Division I schedule."

For Jonas, the conversation had to be bittersweet. He was a young man on a crusade, coming off of a fantastic victory and wanting nothing more than to play for the Tar Heels. At that moment, he clearly didn't want to hear about postponing things for another year. He winced, slightly.

Immediately recognizing that he had taken the wind out of Jonas' sails, Vogle asked him to let the idea sink in.

"Obviously, we don't need an answer right now. You've got plenty of time to think this through. We'll be sending a written invitation in the next few weeks. After you get it, and have had time to discuss it with your coach, your teachers and your aunt and uncle; we can talk some more."

Smiling broadly, Vogle shook Jonas' hand and said good-bye. The young player managed a weak grin, while Hank, euphoric over the victory and thrilled to have a UNC coach speaking to one of his players, grabbed Vogle's hand, pumping it vigorously. As Freddie pulled away, Hank turned and put his arm around Jonas' shoulder, bellowing, "Great game, Son. Now, go get yourself a shower."

Standing within earshot, but just outside of the group, I thought, "God, Hank's going to be unbearable now; mentor and father figure to the young Baltic sensation. I hope that he doesn't screw it up for Jonas." Still needing to get taped comments, I stepped up, offering Hank my congratulations.

"Tremendous victory, Coach," I said as I put the mike up to Stoddard's face. "How do you break it down?'

"Great, hard-nosed basketball; simply great, hard-nosed basketball. Durham has outstanding players, but we persevered and came out on top. We almost let it get away from us there at the end, but our guys showed that they've learned the lessons

I've preached all year long. They relied on the fundamentals stressed so hard every day in practice. It was a great step forward for the program I've been building since I got here; and a great victory for Carolina high school basketball. Thanks to your station for covering us all year and thanks to our great fans. Now, I've got to get to the locker room and be with my kids."

Having delivered his platitudes and grabbing more credit than he deserved for the game's outcome, Hank turned and headed away. But I still needed a quote about Jonas.

"Hank," I called out. "Do you have anything to say about Jonas?"

Realizing that he had ignored the goose that laid the golden egg, Hank turned back towards me, again approaching the mike.

"I love the kid. He's a great young man and a special talent. I can't say enough about him. He's only been here a few months, but we've grown so close."

"Thanks, Coach, and what about his play to pull out the win?"

"That play was fantastic. It showed that he's absorbing everything I can offer him. He's soaking it up like a sponge."

With that, Hank turned and headed to the locker room.

"Bullshit," I thought. "The only thing 'taught' about what we just witnessed is what Jonas taught himself; when the game is on the line great players have to step up."   Finished with Hank, I headed to the lobby phone booth to file my report. A technician at the station would tape my comments and splice in a few of the coaches' statements that I played to him, creating a coherent segment for play throughout the remainder of the evening and the following morning.

While entering the phone booth and reaching into my pocket for a dime, I spotted Olivia standing at the gym's outside entrance. Although she was facing in my direction, she didn't see me, as she was fully engaged in conversation. Initially, I didn't notice who she was talking to because I was preoccupied with dialing WTHL. But while the station phone was ringing, I glanced out from the booth and got a good look at her companion. It was the old guy in the black suit.

Chapter 5
Moe

By the time I finished filing my piece with the station, the old stranger had once again disappeared. Olivia spotted me exiting the booth, crossed the lobby and gave me a kiss.

"Are you happy with your story?" she asked.

"It's not bad, but maybe not quite up to the game of the decade. Coach Olson gave Jonas the credit he deserved, but I had a hard time getting Hank to remember that it wasn't all about him."

"Let's not spoil a fantastic evening by talking about Hank."

"OK, let's switch to the older man in your life. Who's the guy in black? I keep seeing him everywhere?"

"Oh, you caught us. I knew you'd be jealous, but you've got nothing to worry about. He's very suave, but he's old enough to be my grandfather. Besides, I'm not crazy about the way he dresses, and he's not nearly as cute as you."

"Good. I feel so much better. But seriously, who is he?"

"Wish I could tell you, but I really don't know. We chatted for about fifteen minutes. He was charming, but he didn't tell me all that much about himself. His name is Morris. He said that I could call him 'Moe.' He lives somewhere near New York City, and said that he travels a lot. He's visiting the area. Other than that, we talked about the game. He's obviously into sports. He said that he loves a good game, and that some of the finest moments of his life have been spent at sporting events. He raved about Jonas, especially the fact that he's European. But he also complimented the other players on both teams. He wasn't too impressed with Hank, though."

"Hey, I'm starting to like him."

"On the other hand, he did say that he liked my smile and my outfit. I got the impression that maybe he was trying to pick me up, so I made a reference to you as my 'boyfriend' and said that you were probably calling in your story. The next thing you know, the conversation got a little awkward. He said that he would like to meet you sometime, but that he had a prior appointment; and then he was gone."

"A geriatric, man of mystery. Did he mention his last name?"

"He did, but I didn't quite catch it. I think it begins with a 'B'. Bird? Burke? Something like that, but more Jewish-sounding."

"Berg? Did he say, Berg?"

"Yeah. That's it. 'Berg.' Moe Berg."

"Whoa! That's Moe Berg, the Moe Berg. I knew I'd seen him somewhere before. His picture shows up in a lot of articles covering old timers' events. He's a baseball legend."

"So, he was a great ballplayer?"

"Hell no. He wasn't great at all, but he had staying power. He lasted something like fifteen years as a reserve catcher, playing in the twenties and thirties. He was slow and only hit about two forty-something, but he was a good fielder and he handled pitchers really well."

"That sounds like a lot of guys. What made him a legend?."

"He's freakin' brilliant. For a ballplayer, he's something of a genius. He speaks seven languages, maybe more. He went to Princeton, back before Jews were usually allowed into Princeton. He got a law degree from Columbia, studied philosophy at the Sorbonne, and was a big prize winner on some radio quiz show."

"Pretty impressive."

"Yeah, the sports writers loved him. He got a ton of coverage just because he was so different, a true intellectual jock."

"And he tried to pick me up! Now, I'll have something to tell our grandchildren."

"Yeah, but there's even more."

"More?"

"He was a spy."

"A spy!"

"Uh huh. I read somewhere that he served in the O.S.S. during World War II. If so, that would probably make him a spy."

"What's the O.S.S.?"

"It doesn't exist anymore, but it was the Office of Strategic Services, the forerunner of the CIA. As I understand it, the O.S.S. was jump-started at the beginning of World War II because the U.S. didn't really have an intelligence operation; so, they built one from scratch. They recruited ultra-smart people to do things like break codes and infiltrate behind enemy lines. Because the O.S.S. was so new, the agents had a lot of freedom to do their own thing. I think that Berg was placed in Europe during the war, and I know that he toured Japan with Babe Ruth while he was still playing baseball in the thirties. Who knows, he may have been spying back then. The guy speaks so many languages that he could have gathered intelligence data practically anywhere."

"I don't like this spying thing. It's not honest. It offends my Quaker sensibilities."

"But you're not a Quaker. You're an agnostic."

"Yes, but I went to a Quaker college, and I work at Quaker

school. Some of their "Integrity Testimony" has rubbed off, probably through osmosis. There's something about spying that doesn't sit right. What kind of person leads a double life? How can you trust someone who's been involved in so many lies?"

"You've got me. I've never known a spy before."

"Are you sure? A spy wouldn't tell you that he or she is a spy."

"Hmm, I never thought about it. You're not a spy are you?"

"No."

"How do I know?"

"You'll just have to trust me."

"OK. I trust you. I even love you. Can we go home and go to bed now?"

" You really have a one-track mind, don't you."

"Yes."

"That's not good."

"But I'm honest. You can trust me."

"Ok, you win. Trust conquers all. Let's go home."

* * * * * *

Although I hadn't pulled weekend duty at Carlson, I had several major assignments due before the start of spring break, which was only a few weeks away. Also, Olivia needed some time to herself to grade papers and plan her classes for the upcoming week. So, after a leisurely Saturday morning brunch, I headed back to the dorm in order to put in a good six hours at my typewriter before meeting Olivia for dinner at the Rathskeller, a downtown Chapel Hill haunt, and going to an 8:00 PM showing of *The Godfather* at the Carolina Theater.

Upon entering Carlson, I noticed that Suzie was once again working at the desk. Figuring that Moe Berg had probably struck up a conversation with her a few days earlier, when I had spotted him in the lobby, I decided to see what, if anything, she had learned about the old ball player. As I approached the counter, I could see that Suzie was watching a mid-day news break on the office TV. The coverage was of more Vietnam casualty body bags being delivered to Dover Air Force Base. Against this solemn scene, the broadcaster announced that President Nixon was promising to reduce U.S. troop strength by seventy thousand.

"So,Suzy, what's new at the ranch?"

"Well, another Russian has checked in. He's on Joe's floor in one of the rooms just above your suite."

"No kidding. All of a sudden Carlson is a Russian magnet. What's this guy's story?"

"His name is Nikolai Andropov and he's been accepted into the Public Administration master's program, but the word circulating through the RA staff is that he's been sent here to watch over Vladi. Tony's already nicknamed him "KGB."

It's pretty creepy. He wears a trench coat. He's got this close-cropped military haircut. He's always smoking, and he hold's his cigarettes funny. You know, like this."

Suzy held up an imaginary cigarette between her thumb and her forefinger, taking a deep drag and looking exaggeratingly mysterious.

"Just another nut in the nuthouse," I quipped. "And there's been another character that's been hanging around. Have you talked to the old guy in the black suit?'

"You mean Moe?"

"Yeah, Moe? What's the scoop on Moe?"

"He's quite the flirt, a seventy-something ladies-man. He stopped by the desk one day to ask for some directions, picked up on my accent and we started chatting about New York City. It's incredible, Eck, he knows everything about the city. Anyway, he's already asked me out to dinner, twice. And I think I'm going to take him up on it, cause I'll be able to spend the evening practicing my French. He's amazingly fluent. "

"You sure that you want to do that? You think you'll be safe?"

"It's not like I plan to go back to his room with him or anything. I'll meet him up on Franklin Street. We'll eat at the Carolina Coffee Shop; then we'll say,'Ouvroir.'"

"Where's he staying?"

"He's on campus at the Carolina Inn."

"Do you know what brought him here?"

"He said that he's living in North Jersey, just outside of New York, but that he's traveled his whole adult life and needs to get out on the road to enjoy himself. He likes Chapel Hill because it's a pretty place to walk - he loves to walk; we don't get much snow; and the weather is easier on his joints than New York's. He plans to hang around until just after the Yankees pass through at the end of March on their way north to start the season. They're going to play some sort of exhibition game with the Tar Heels, which should be fun. He knows the owner and has a block of seats right behind the dugout. He's already asked me to go with him, and to bring some of my friends. Do you and Olivia want to go to? "

"You're on. I'll probably be covering the game for the station anyway, but sitting with Moe Berg, how cool is that!"

"And speaking of the Devil, take a look behind you ."

I glanced over my shoulder and there, entering the lobby, was Moe, dressed as usual in his worn black suit and overcoat. Spotting Suzy at the desk, Moe headed straight towards her. While still a good ten yards away, he called out to her,

"The dinner invitation still stands, My Dear. How about tonight at 6:00?"

"It's a date," chirped Suzy. "The Carolina Coffee Shop at 6:00. I'll meet you there. By the way, this is my friend and fellow

RA, Eckhardt Larsen. He's a pretty big fan of yours, Moe."

"You must be a real connoisseur of the game, if you're a fan of mine. "

"I guess you could say that," I answered. "It sounds a lot better than being called a 'sports junkie,' which is what most people call me."

"My Boy, athletics are a noble endeavor, a civilized substitute for naked human aggression involving unique syntheses of skill and strategy. To acquire a rich knowledge of sports is to become finely attuned to some of our great accomplishments as a species."

I felt my own self-concept improving with just this small dose of the vaunted Moe Berg eloquence and charm. Then, turning on a dime, he delivered his punch-line in a savvy New York accent.

"Listen, Kid, I know how ya feel. My old man never forgave me for becoming a ball player. But, what the hell did he know. Just tell em, 'Up your's' and keep on doin' what you love to do. It'll carry you a long way."

I was hooked. The guy was an intellectual with street smarts. No wonder the sports writers had loved him. So, after Moe determined that Suzy was not available to take a walk with him, I jumped at the chance to accompany him on a foot tour of the campus. My course assignments could wait. This was the chance of a lifetime.

As we continued chatting at the information desk, across the lobby the elevator door opened and out stepped Vladi and Janine. It was now the first week of March and Chapel Hill was experiencing one of those early spring days that begin teasing out the dogwood and rosebud blossoms. The sun was shining with the temperature in the mid-sixties. Vladi was clad in checked Bermuda shorts, a flowered, short-sleeved, Hawaiian shirt, and flip flops; while Janine wore black slacks and a

Carolina Blue, cotton sweater over a white blouse. They strolled arm-in-arm across the lobby and out the door, heading towards the heart of the campus. Within moments of their departure, the elevator doors again opened revealing someone I'd never seen before, but who I surmised must be Nikolai Andropov, a.k.a. "KGB." As Suzy had predicted, he was wearing a grey trench-coat and grasping a cigarette. He appeared to be in his mid-thirties, standing about 5 foot 9 inches, with a powerful, stocky build. As he slid out of the elevator, he stared intently through the entrance doors at Vladi and Janine as they glided up the brick sidewalk away from the dorm. Without bothering to survey the scene inside, he swiftly moved across the lobby and out the front doors, following the two at a safe distance.

Suzy, Moe and I all observed this scene, but none of us commented on it. Instead, Moe quipped, "Well, I have a much anticipated dinner date tonight. In order to get showered and get a little nap beforehand, we'd better get started on our walk, Mr. Larsen."

"Ok, Moe. Let's go." And bidding Suzy farewell, we, too, headed out of the dorm.

Moe had a remarkably strong gait for someone in his early seventies, who had played 15 years in the majors, primarily at catcher. I had a little trouble keeping up with him.

"Looks like your knees are holding up pretty well," I commented, breathing heavily.

"Not bad at all, Mr. Larsen. The secret is to not play in too many games."

We proceeded past the other dorms and towards scenic Keenan Stadium, where the Tar Heels play their football games. Moe regaled me with the broad strokes and some of the details of his baseball career. I knew a few of the facts already; but I listened carefully, recognizing that in my entire life I might never get another chance like this. He explained that after playing shortstop at Princeton and graduating magna cum laude, he signed with the Brooklyn Dodgers in 1923. Then, he bounced around the minors for a few years, while working on his law degree and also studying in Paris; after which, he was signed by the White Sox. He stumbled into playing catcher when all three catchers on the team got hurt at the same time. He displayed a knack for fielding behind the plate and he also had a "rifle arm." His hitting started coming around too. In fact, in 1929, as the team's regular catcher, he appeared in 106 games, batted 288 and received two votes for the league's MVP award. But the next spring he suffered a knee injury that set him back the rest of his career, slowing down his running and moving him into the reserve niche that he would fill with the Cleveland Indians, Washington Senators and Boston Red Sox. He retired at 37 in 1939, and tried coaching for a few years with the Red Sox before getting out of the game altogether.

"You know," Moe added. "With the current diluted talent pool, spread over so many teams; if I had been playing today, I could have probably lasted until my early forties. How many teams these days would turn up their noses at a great fielding catcher with a .243 lifetime batting average?"

"None," I answered, on cue.

"Correct response, Mr. Larsen. Correct response. But life is fickle and it conspired to pull me away from the game. Coaching wasn't all that bad. I might even have stayed in it long enough to become a manager, but The War intervened. The urge to serve was too great."

"So, is that when you became a spy, or did you start back in your playing days ?" I asked, deciding to move the conversation into riskier territory.

"A spy, hmm. How much do you know about all of that?"

"I read somewhere that when you toured Japan with Babe Ruth and Lou Gehrig, you secretly took movies of the Tokyo skyline that were later used to plan the wartime bombing of the city. I also ran across some stories reporting that you served in the O.S.S. during the war and speculating that you were with the CIA well into the fifties. That's about all that I know. "

"There are several chapters to the saga. How much time do you have?"

"What is it now, about 1:30? Like you, I'm on for dinner at 6:00. We've got time to burn," I said as we strolled by the Old Well at the heart of the campus and began heading towards Franklin Street and Chapel Hill's quaint, downtown "village"

"Ok, I'm going to tell you some things about those years, Mr. Larsen. The fact of the matter is that I probably don't have too much time left on this earth and there isn't much reason for secrecy any more. Even more importantly, Eckhardt, I need your help with something, and I think that I can trust you. But more about that later."

My heart skipped a beat at the mention of Moe needing my help. " What in the hell am I getting myself into?" I wondered. But I plunged ahead anyway, not seriously giving any consideration to cutting Moe off. "Great," I offered. "I'm all ears."

As we walked west along Franklin Street towards the adjoining town of Carrboro, Moe shared fantastic stories about his war experiences with the O.S.S.

"The Japanese films were taken under my own initiative. It was apparent to me by the late thirties that their military machine was likely to pose a threat to the United States. So, I saw an opportunity to gather some useful information, and I took it. It was serendipitous, really; and it helped to open doors for me later when the O.S.S. was formed."

"It was a dangerous time, Eckhardt. The United States had never had a full-time, professional spy organization before, and we were pretty much winging it. We recruited smart people to break codes and analyze complex intelligence data. Speaking multiple languages was essential, if you were going behind enemy lines; and those of us who did so were given remarkable latitude to go wherever we chose and gather whatever information we considered important. It was a freewheeling era, driven by the tragic necessity of war."

Moe told me about several close scrapes, and one torrid love affair in Italy prior to Mussolini's fall. He gave a detailed account of his most important mission, infiltrating a scientific conference in Zurich, Switzerland to assess the likelihood of the Germans developing an atomic bomb.

"I was charged with assassinating Werner Heisenberg, the lead scientist on the German A-bomb project. Following his presentation of a scientific paper, I managed to take a lengthy walk with Heisenberg and question him in great detail. Fortunately for both of us, it became clear to me that the Germans didn't have the capacity to produce the bomb."

"Both of you?"

"Yes, both of us. I would have killed him, because so much was at stake; but I liked Heisenberg and I really didn't want to shoot him. Also, I'm not sure that I could have made it out of their alive."

We walked for several miles around the Chapel Hill and Carborro business districts and the adjoining residential areas, then began heading in the direction of the Carolina Inn on the northwest edge of the campus. Suddenly, Moe's tone changed, his voice taking on a far more serious tone.

"Eckhardt, I'll be frank with you. I left the CIA in the fifties, when the bureaucrats and bean counters gained control. But I've taken selected 'contract jobs' jobs ever since; nothing very big, but always matters worth keeping under surveillance to prevent them from getting out of control and possibly creating crises."

"In this business, it's necessary sometimes to take risks, putting your trust in carefully selected individuals. Your own life and the lives of others can depend on such people. Eckhardt, I've decided that you are such an individual, which is why I'm sharing with you that I'm here on a CIA assignment."

"Oh, Man. You're shittin' me," I gasped as soon as Moe paused.

"Eckhardt, I'm too old and this business is too important for me to be 'shitting you.' By even mentioning to you that I'm on a mission, I've crossed the Rubicon. You are now 'in' and really have no choice but to cooperate, as you'll better understand once I explain things to you in more detail. "

I quickly found myself wishing that I had never agreed to the walk with the old spy. "What in the hell is going on? I'm screwed." I worried.

"Now, I know that you're probably wondering what you have gotten yourself into," Moe stated dryly, as though anticipating my every thought . "So, let me give you some important, additional information. This out-of-the-way corner of the world, your so-called 'Carolina Blue Heaven,' has either serendipitously, or by insidious design, attracted two highly talented individuals from behind the Iron Curtain. First, the young basketball phenomenon, Petraitis, and now the poet, Borzov, have found their way here. This, of course, has drawn the attention of both the KGB and the CIA; which is why the agent, Andropov, whose real name happens to be Ivanovich, has appeared on your doorstep, as have I."

"Seems like a series of coincidences to me," I offered .

"You may well be correct, my young friend, but even clear-headed, detached observers can sometimes look at coincidences and see conspiracies. There is no denying that they both defected at similar times. Also, there is no denying that they landed within 15 miles of each other. Might it not be possible that someone, or some group, had a hand in this? Might more defections loom on the horizon? The Soviets let no high-profile coincidences go uninvestigated. It's the nature of dictatorships to ferret out conspiracies before they gain momentum. And sometimes, even when a conspiracy doesn't exist, it's deemed prudent to make an example of innocent individuals caught up in coincidences. Such "examples" enhance the fear that undergirds dictatorial control."

"Examples?"

"Yes, 'examples.' To put it more bluntly, the KGB might decide that this situation requires that someone, either Petraitis or Borzov – perhaps both - be eliminated in order to send a message to the populace that flight, and embarrassing the state, is not a viable option."

"Jesus, you're not kidding, are you?"

"I'm not remotely close to kidding, Eckhardt. This is very serious business."

"So, why me? What do you want from me?"

"Regarding 'Why you?' The answer is chance, Eckhardt, sheer chance. Because of your position in Carlson Dorm and your relationship with Olivia Russell – a lovely young woman, by the way – you are the one person situated at the nexus of the possible Petraitis – Borzov connection."

"Moe, they don't even know each other, I interrupted. "They haven't even met."

"Then why was Borzov at the game last night?

"Hell, I told Vladi and Janine that it was going to be a great game and that they ought to try to take it in. It's just another coincidence."

"Like I told you, Eckhardt, you sit at the intersection of this situation and innocent acts on your part can have unintended effects for the other participants, and for the perceptions of outside observers. Now, back to your question about what I would like you to do. I want you to help me monitor the situation. You are in a much better position than I to report on the actions of Borzov, Petraitis and the KGB agent, Andropov. Given what you have already told me, it's Andropov who is causing me the most concern. If there is any indication that he might make a move on either Borzov or Petraitis, I may need to preempt him. "

"Preempt him?"

"He might have to be sacrificed, Eckhardt. We can't allow KGB agents to assassinate people here in the U.S."

"So, how in the hell am I going to know if he intends to assassinate one of them?"

"Good question. You can't be certain. You have to rely on your instincts in work like this."

"Rely on my instincts about whether or not you should kill someone. Moe, you're crazy. You want me to give you the heads up to wipe someone out?"

"My boy, the harsh reality is that you're not going to have a choice. Events beyond your control will force you to act. You are a person of conscience, and you won't be willing to stand by and watch an innocent person – or innocent people – get hurt, maybe killed."

As Moe finished delivering his message, we arrived at the Carolina Inn. Standing in front of the entrance, he reached for my hand, into which he pressed a small piece of paper. "Here's my room number, along with the Carolina Inn phone number. All I am asking is that you watch carefully, and if you see anything that causes you to be suspicious that Andropov is going to go beyond merely keeping Borzov and Petraitis under surveillance, alert me immediately. Call and ask to talk to me. If I don't answer the phone, leave a message at the desk. Make it sufficiently cryptic, so the desk attendant won't be alarmed. I'll be checking with the desk, regularly, so no message will go too long without me learning about it. Again, all you have to do is alert me that something is possibly afoot. I'll take over from there, determining the seriousness of the matter and the steps that must be taken. Trust me, Eckhardt. I'm trusting you."

Then, flashing a fatherly smile, Moe turned and headed into the inn, adding, "Time for me to grab a catnap before my dinner date. Cheers."

"Cheers!" I muttered to myself as I began walking across campus to the dorm. "There's nothin' cheery about any of this. What am I going to do? "

Then came an "Aha!" moment and a sudden wave or relief. "Christ, he's probably not working for the CIA. The old guy's delusional. This can't be real. It's just too far out. Go back to the dorm, wash up, and get downtown to dinner with Olivia. Just stay calm, Eck, all you need to do to get back in touch with reality is to talk to some people who are sane."

I picked up my pace and began jogging back to Carlson.

Chapter 6
Eavesdropping

By the time I reached the dorm, I was satisfied that there was nothing to worry about. But then I bumped into Wolf – our reclusive, computer engineer RA -   who had replaced Suzy at the information desk. "Hey, what's up, Wolfman?

"Up? Lots of things could be 'up.' Do you have any particular domain of 'up' options in mind?"

"Ok let me narrow it down it a bit. How about the Carlson domain? What's up around Carlson, Mr. Elder Student?"

"It's timely that you should ask, Eck. There is some very heavy stuff that's 'up'in Carlson, as we speak."

"Heavy stuff, huh. What's happening that's so heavy?"

"KGB's 'up' to somethin'."

"Alright, ever since he walked in the door, everybody's been saying that KGB's 'up' to something. So, what's KGB 'up' to? "

"Not quite sure, but I don't think that it's somethin' good. He's been talkin' to the Soviet embassy, gettin' some kind of marchin' orders."

"And how might you know this? "

"Cause Jonathan" (the assistant residence director) "and I tapped his phone,"

"You what?" I shouted.

"For God sake, Eck. Lower the volume. Don't go gettin' us in trouble."

"We're the only ones in sight, Wolfie." I shot back defensively. "First of all, it's illegal for you to tap a phone, But, second, how do you even know how to do it?" I whispered.

"Hell, Eck, I've been livin' here for over twelve years now, and I'm the resident computer and electronics guru. There's nothin' about this dorm that I don't know. Got any more dumb questions?"

"You win. So what have you unearthed?"

"Like I told you. He's talkin' to the Soviet embassy and their tellin' him what they want him to do. But we can't figure out just what it is cause they'll be talkin' along in Russian and then they suddenly break into some kind of coded gibberish that we haven't cracked yet. But we'll get it. It's just a matter of time."

"Wait a minute. These guys are talking in Russian. So how are you making any sense out of what they're saying to begin with?"

"No problem when you can draw on Carlson's collective genius. We make tapes and then have Charlotte translate them for us. She's our own in-house Slavic languages queen."

Just then, Joe got off of the elevator and headed towards the front desk.

"Hey, Big Guy, where you been? As if I don't know. How's Olivia?

"Olivia's fine, just fine, Joe."

"Good, so what you guy's doin'?"

"Shhh, Joe. Don't draw attention to us." I scolded.

"There's nobody in the whole damned lobby, but us." Joe retorted, shooting me a "you're so pathetic" look.

"Nobody that we can see, but that doesn't mean that there aren't cameras and microphones hidden around here." I said with my hand shielding the side of my face and masking my voice.

"Oh, gettin' a little paranoid about KGB, I see."

"There's nothing paranoid about this, Joe. Vladi's being watched and there could be trouble ahead. We've got to warn him."

"And what makes you think that he doesn't already know?"

"What do you mean?"

"I mean that, as Janine's been telling me, Vladi is hip to KGB. He's used to being followed. He was followed in the Soviet Union all the time, and he knows that he's being followed here. He's even talked to KGB about it. He asked him why it took him so long to show up."

"Okay, good point, but Wolfie thinks that maybe somethin' is 'up.' He's been tapping KGB's phone, and he thinks that he may be getting ready to make some sort of move. You never know, he might be ordered to erase Vladi."

"Could be, but that wouldn't come as any shock to Vladi. Janine says that for years he's figured that he's been living on borrowed time. Being a dissident in the Soviet Union ain't for the faint-hearted, Big Guy."

"So, let me get this right. You're saying that we don't have to tell Vladi?"

"Well, not unless you've got something new to tell. He's way ahead of all of us about this stuff. Do you know anything specific, Wolfowitz?"

"Now that you put it that way; no, we don't. We're workin' on it, but we don't have anything that we can pin on KGB. "

"Why don't we do this." Joe offered, showing far greater wisdom than I would have ever expected from him. "I'll tell Janine, with whom I'm growing increasingly close, that we're all doing our best to cover Vladi's back. I'll say that we've got our eyes and ears open; and if it looks like something bad is in the works, we'll let him know right away and call in the FBI. What do you think?"

"I can't think of anything better." I answered. "That work for you, Wolfman?"

"As good as anything. I'll pass it on to Jonathan and Charlotte."

"But on a more important front, Amigo, just how close are you and Janine?"

"Well, Eck, let's just say that she doesn't spend all of her time with Vladi. And Vladi doesn't spend all of his time with her. It seems that they have an 'open' relationship, and Janine's already been 'open' to working on her tennis game. Once it warms up, we're looking at a trip down to Wrightsville Beach to teach her how to surf."

"And what about the physical side of your relationship, Mr. Conquistador?"

"No wine before its time, Eck. No wine before it's time? We have the rest of our lives ahead of us."

"Sounds to me like you're slowing down, maybe losing your touch. But then, maybe she's just making an upstanding man out of you. Maybe she's 'The One.'"

"Don't go broadcasting anything over the radio just yet, Eck. How can there be just 'One' when there are still so many women and so little time?"

* * * * * *

Things remained pretty much status quo for the next six weeks. Vladi, with Janine translating, gave weekly lectures in the UNC Comparative Literature program. The rest of his time was spent prowling around Chapel Hill or holed up in his room, presumably writing poetry and/or frolicking with Janine, who managed to break free now and then, appearing with Joe on the

Carlson tennis courts. I'd spot him standing directly behind her, his body snug against hers, both of them grasping her racket, as he showed her how to stroke a forehand. Or he would place both arms around her, as he demonstrated how to grip a two-handed backhand.

Meanwhile, KGB appeared to be attending his classes. Otherwise, he spent most of his time at the dorm or tagging along, at a safe distance, after Vladi.

As for Moe, he began hanging around the dorm more frequently and extended his stay in town well beyond the Yankee's visit to Chapel Hill. Moe soon became something of a celebrity around Carlson, mesmerizing anyone who would listen to him with his baseball stories and travelogues. Discussion of his spying experiences, however, remained taboo. As far as I could tell, he never leaked a word to anyone but me.

By the end of March, the high school and NCAA basketball seasons both came to a close. Jonas, who led HFA to the independent school state championship, was selected MVP of the state tournament. Although offered scholarships at two less prestigious, mid-major basketball schools, Ohio University and Marshall; he stayed true to his dream, opting for a post-graduate year at HFA and the potential UNC scholarship. The Tarheels, meanwhile, went 26 and 5, winning the ACC regular season and tournament championships, only to lose to the Florida State Seminoles by four points in a semi-final game of the Final Four. The Seminoles subsequently lost a close championship game to one of John Wooden's great UCLA teams. Bill Walton was chosen tournament MVP.

* * * * * *

That's how things stood in mid-April when Maxine - our Vietnam vet , physical activity freak, medical student, RA -

organized a Saturday canoe trip down a twelve-mile stretch of the Haw, the scenic river located just south of Chapel Hill, towards Pittsboro. While trolling Carlson's lobby on Friday afternoon, still looking for residents to sign up, she came across Joe and me lounging on a lobby sofa.

"You guys up for tomorrow's river trip of a lifetime?"

"For it to be the river trip of my lifetime, it's got to be you and me naked in a kayak," Joe quipped.

"Dream on, JoJo. I'll share a canoe with you, but I'd snuggle up to any of several Viet Cong I've met before I'd get naked with you."

"You really know how to hurt a guy, Max."

"So, who's signed up?" I asked.

"It's looking like its going to be pretty much a staff excursion. The only residents that I've managed to corral are Janine and Vladi, which of course means that KGB has signed up too. I've got him sharing a canoe with Rev. Al.'

"Whoa, you got the Residence Director to go along. Rack up points for you." Joe slipped in. "What other staff are going?"

"Well, Scott and Hillary will be our undergraduate contingent. And Castelli and Suzy will share a canoe."

Just then, Jonathan, the Assistant Residence Director, strolled by.

"Hey, Jack, you up for Maxine's canoe trip?" I asked.

"Hell no. I don't do canoes. Besides, my lady is flying in from Ann Arbor." (Jonathan's fiancée was a grad student at Michigan.) "And I'm in charge while Rev. Al is out there on the river with you guys, the snakes and the mosquitoes. Have fun."

"Hey, we haven't committed yet," quipped Joe

But I already knew that I'd be going. If Vladi and KGB were going to be out there on the river together, I was going to have to monitor the situation. Moe was right. I'd gotten sucked in and I was determined to keep Vladi safe as long as my "watch" at

Carlson lasted.

"You can count us in," I said   "Joe and I are good on the water. But, if he's going to share a canoe with you, I'm going to need a partner. Olivia already told me that I have to fend for myself because she has to grade papers all weekend.'

"Not-to-worry,   Eck. I'll match you up with someone." Maxine quipped. "In fact, I just got off of the phone with Lovely Lisa a few minutes ago. She wasn't sure she was going to go because she didn't have a partner, but she's might be up for sharing a canoe with you."

"What are you trying to do, Max, get me into divorce court before I'm even married?   Lisa is a sexy, slinky, jealousy generator."

"Relax, Eck. Olivia can handle it. I already talked it over with her."

"Even before you knew that I was going. Why didn't you tell me?"

"I knew that I could count on you. Believe me, she's fine with it. She's a strong, secure woman, who knows that she's got you wrapped around her little finger."

"Ok, ok. I'm whipped. I know it, but you don't have to rub it in. So, what time are we shoving off on this great adventure?"

"A little bit later than I'd like. I've got to run around to a couple of places first thing in the morning to gather up enough canoes. We'll meet in the dorm parking lot at 10:00 AM. I'll have my truck, a trailer and the canoes.   Bring your own sandwiches and drinks, preferably something soft. I don't need any drunken paddlers."

"You don't have to worry about us. We don't mix alcohol and water sports," inserted Joe. "That's for afterwards."

"Sounds good, fellas. See you in the morning."

Wanting to make sure that this was cool with Olivia, I gave her a call at home soon after school let out.

"Hi, Honey. "

"Hey, Larsen , What's up? You still coming over for dinner?"

"Sure, but I wanted to touch base with you about this canoe trip that Maxine pulled together for tomorrow."

"Yeah, what a great idea. I'm really stoked for you. Check out the Haw, so we can go by ourselves later in the spring. I haven't done a river trip since Hoover, and it's been too long."

During college, Olivia had been a counselor at Camp Lou Henry Hoover, a Girl Scout camp near the Delaware Water Gap in New Jersey. Each year she led a trip of seven or eight canoes down the Delaware River from Port Jervis, New York to Columbia, New Jersey, a trip of nearly 50 miles involving modest rapids.

"You're sure you want me to go, even though you're not going to be there?"

"Of course, why wouldn't I?"

"You're sure that you want me to go, even though Max is pairing me up in the same canoe with Lisa?"

"Should I be concerned?"

"Of course not, you're much more intelligent and sexy than she is, and I only have eyes for you."

"Good response, almost convincing. But the truth is I just have to trust you, Larsen. I've got so much work to do that I can't possibly go; and our relationship wouldn't be worth much if I couldn't trust you. Now would it?"

"That's why I love you. You've got the whole situation, including me, all figured out. I'll be over in about an hour for supper, what should I bring?"

"You pick up the wine and some bread. I've got the rest."

"Great. See you soon."

Olivia whipped up some gazpacho and shrimp-fried rice, with some bacon mixed in. I threw together a salad, and we sat out on her back deck, eating by candlelight. We passed on desert at home, opting for a walk to downtown Hillsborough for ice cream at the old drug store's soda fountain. It couldn't have been better. But as we were approaching the center of town, Olivia broke the spell.

"I've got a surprise for you. When we talked about the canoe trip, it sounded like so much fun that I decided, 'Screw the work for once, I'm going to go.' I called Maxine. It's all working out fine. And, by the way, it's not that I don't trust you. I trust you more than anything. It's just that the weather is supposed to be great tomorrow and I want to share the trip with you. I should be the one making the memories with you, instead of Lisa."

"Sounds great to me. Did Maxine dig up someone to paddle along with Lisa?"

"No, I did?"

"Who'd you find on such short notice, somebody from your department?

"Nope. Guess again."

"Hank. You decided to hook him up with Lisa, and then her two stalkers will take care of him."

"Interesting idea, but not even close. One more guess."

"You've got me. I'm clueless. Who'd you find?"

And then she dropped the bomb.

"Jonas."

"Jonas!"

"Yes, Jonas. He's really excited to be going with us."

"Yeah, well, trust me on this. I don't think that he should go."

"You're kidding. Why not?"

"I've got a funny feeling about it."

"What's that supposed to mean?"

"I just don't feel good about it."

"And I repeat, what's that mean? The weather forecast is great. We've got nothing else planned. I love canoeing. I've talked to Jonas, and so does he. You and I have talked about getting out on a river for a long time. It's only a twelve-mile stretch. What's the problem?"

"You're right about all of those things, Olivia, all of them. But there's something about getting my two Russians and your Lithuanian in close proximity on the water that worries me. Why did you have to go and invite Jonas? And how do we go about uninviting him?"

As soon as the words were out of my mouth, I knew that I shouldn't have said them.

"Well since you asked," Olivia curtly responded. " I invited Jonas because he's a fine, mature, lonely, young man, who needs some good clean fun around young adults, who he relates to far better than the high school kids fate has assigned him to."

"Christ, Olivia, He'll be sharing a canoe with Lisa. She'll relate to him alright."

"Listen, Eck. he's already 19 going on 25. He can take care of himself. And I'll tell Lisa to back off, if you want. But what's this thing about "your" Russians? Why are you worried about them?"

I had never come clean with Olivia about Moe's revelation, now substantiated by Wolf, that KGB really was a Soviet agent. I'd thought about it every day, but always kept it to myself, rationalizing that Olivia would worry constantly about everyone's safety. Maybe I was too patronizing. Maybe I shouldn't have been trying to protect her; but Moe didn't want me blabbing any of this around. I was sure that if I told Olivia, I'd be on the slippery slope to telling others. And who knows, Olivia just might let it slip too.

But then, it all came flooding out.

"Olivia, believe me, there's some real danger here."

"I know. I know canoeing, better than you. I understand the danger."

"I'm not talking about that kind of danger. I'm talking about KGB actually being a Soviet agent who is spying on both Vladi and Jonas; a spy who may have orders to kill either, or both, of them at any time."

The color drained from Olivia's face.

"You're making this up. You're joking, right?"

"Nope. I wish I was. Moe told me. And Wolf has hard evidence on KGB. We're caught up in something big, something big and scary."

"So, what…what…what are we going to do, Larsen?"

"How about if we start by having Jonas *not* go on this canoe trip."

"Eckhard, I promised him. He's really excited about this. Can we keep KGB from going instead?"

" I suppose that's an option. But I'm clueless about how we might pull it off. Any ideas?"

"Yeah, I have an idea."

"What?"

"I think that maybe we're working ourselves into a frenzy when we shouldn't be. I mean KGB is going to be surrounded by people in canoes. Why would he possibly try something out on the Haw in the middle of a flotilla of witnesses? It just doesn't make any sense."

"Yeah, I know. I thought about that. But I can't help worrying. Moe put the fear of God into me."

"I think it's going to be okay, Larsen. Your just a little jumpy from having to keep this to yourself. Let's get our ice cream and go home and go to bed. We have a big day in store for us tomorrow."

Chapter Seven
The Haw

Maxine was a stickler about punctuality. So, at 9:50 AM on Saturday morning everyone was in the Carlson parking lot, decked out in sneakers, shorts, t-shirts and baseball caps; ready to caravan to the spot where we'd be putting into the Haw. Everyone that is except for Vladi and Janine, who seemingly hadn't managed to get out of the sack in time. True to form, at 10 o'clock sharp Maxine pulled into the parking lot, driving her pick-up and pulling a trailer with seven canoes packed with paddles and life vests for all. Visibly miffed when she saw that Vladi and Janine hadn't rallied, Maxine snorted, "We'll just go without them." And she began barking out orders to us all regarding the safety precautions that we would be taking, the most important of which was that each canoe had to have at least one experienced river paddler. To ensure this, Maxine had come up with her own canoe assignments, which she informed us were non-negotiable.

"Okay, Scott and Hillary, like I already told you, you'll be together. That holds for Castelli and Suzy, and Eck and Olivia. Jonas, Olivia tells me that you've done whitewater canoeing in East Germany, so I'm assigning you to paddle with Lisa. You'll be in the rear. Rev. Al, since you've mastered the rapids of the Nolichucky in East Tennessee, I'm putting you with KG..., I mean Nikolai. Joe, I was going to put you with Janine and me with Vladi; but since they're not here, it looks like we may have to go together. Remember to keep your hands to yourself, or you're going to regret it."

"I'll try, Captain Max. But I'm not making any promises. I might not be able to control myself."

Just then, Vladi and Janine came scrambling out onto the fourth floor balcony, waving and shouting at us, trying to make sure that we wouldn't leave without them.

"Thank God!" Maxine exclaimed. "The Russian has come to my rescue."

"No complaints from me, Max. I'll make the best of it." Joe shot back, clearly pleased to be sharing a canoe with Janine.

* * * * * *

It took about a half -hour to drive to the spot on the Haw where we would park and launch our canoes. We were approximately six miles northwest of the Route 15 bridge that crosses the river midway between Chapel Hill and Pittsboro. Maxine's plans called for us to paddle to the bridge, then proceed another six miles in order to complete the full, twelve-mile trip. Before we could start, most of us had to wait at the launch spot, while Maxine, Rev Al, Hillary and Castelli took the truck, the trailer and a few cars to the pickup spot

We expected Max and the others to be back within a half-hour, but the time soon passed without any sign of them. Olivia and I were standing around waiting with our fellow river rats in a sandy turnout above the river. When an hour had gone by, we decided to carry our canoe down the overgrown embankment to the river and paddle around a bit, while we continued waiting. I started down the hill holding the front of the canoe, and had taken only a few steps into the high grass when a startled black snake, seemingly about five-foot long, suddenly sprung up in front of me and hurdled wildly down the hill.

"Holy, shit. What in the hell?" I shouted, dropping the front of the canoe and darting back up the hill.

"It's only a black snake, Larsen," cried Olivia, laughing hysterically along with the rest of the crew. "It's probably more scared than you are, but then again, maybe not."

"It's not just a black snake, Olivia. It's a damned big, black snake. And I don't care how scared it is. It just reminded me why I'll be just fine moving north again. Carolina's got too many freakin'snakes for me; copperheads, water moccasins , rattle snakes, coral snakes and big old black snakes hiding in the grass. Man, give me a break."

"Thanks for the entertainment, Eck. Things had gotten a little slow around here." Joe quipped, not the least consolingly.

"Oh, I'm sure you'd have done a lot better than me if that snake had nearly jumped up your shorts. You'd have had a screaming fit."

"Maybe so, Big Guy. Maybe so. But then I had the good sense to not go plunging off into the high grass without checking to see what might be lying there. Now didn't I?"

"Touché, Joe, touché."

* * * * * *

Suitably humiliated and in no mood for further sparring with Joe, I sulked away towards KGB, who was standing alone smoking. The Russian was my only refuge, as he was the only one not openly laughing at me; although even he had a faint smile on his normally inscrutable face.

"So, Nikolai, have you done much canoeing?" I asked, trying to break the ice.

"No," he answered in his heavily accented, yet surprisingly good, English. "But, I like to swim and I enjoy new challenges."

"Well, hopefully, you won't have to swim today. Rev. Al is pretty experienced, so you shouldn't be capsizing. How's your coursework going?"

"Good. I'm doing well and the Public Administration program provides a very different perspective on managing organizations. "

"Different from?"

"Different from what you might encounter in the Soviet Union."

"So, how'd you end up at Carolina, anyway?" I probed, deciding to explore his cover story.

"I defected." He responded, unfazed by the question.

"I figured that was the case. When?"

"About two-years ago. I was in the Army, assigned as a military attaché to the Soviet Embassy in Austria."

"Defecting can't be an easy thing to do. How'd you pull it off."

"The act of defecting is, actually, not all that hard. I simply walked into the Austrian Foreign Ministry building and told the first official that I saw that I would like to defect. They immediately agreed to provide asylum. The West is eager to gain access to individuals from the Soviet military."

"If you don't mind me asking, if it is so easy, why don't more people do it?

"There is a huge sacrifice, Mr. Larsen. You have to be willing to leave everyone behind, your friends, your family. There is a strong likelihood that you will never see any of them again. That is the hard part."

He was sounding remarkably convincing, almost making me believe him. Pressing deeper, I asked "Why'd you decide to make the leap?"

"My parents were both dead.   I had no siblings. I was married, but the relationship was no longer good, not good at all.

Having spent some time in the West, I became intrigued by the possibilities. Life is a mysterious journey, Mr. Larsen. I saw an opportunity and I took it. Had my personal life been going better, I would not have made the same choice."

"I see your point. But what led you from Austria to Carolina?"

"Frankly, my English is much better than my Austrian. When I decided to go to graduate school, I thought that it would be much better for me to work in a language that suits me. Also, as quality universities go, North Carolina is very inexpensive. I can afford it on the little bit of money that I have been able to save over the last two years and some scholarship money that I receive from a foundation that supports people of Russian descent. I have few personal needs, so I am able to make a go of it."

If Moe and Wolf hadn't given me enough evidence to thoroughly convince me that that KGB was a Soviet agent, I'd have been totally taken in by the guy, particularly because his hard exterior softened appreciably as we chatted. Then, completely unexpectedly, he started playing with me.

"But the primary reason that I chose to come to North Carolina is that I am especially fond of pork barbecue. I prefer *pulled* rather than the *sliced.*

"Bullock's in Durham and Allen and Son's just outside of Chapel Hill are both particularly good, and are well known in both the Soviet Union and Austria. How could I go anywhere else!" He said cracking the first broad grin that I'd ever seen from him.

I broke into a laugh and played along. "How about that, we've got ourselves a Russian barbecue freak. God, I love those two spots. We'll have to go together sometime."

"Perhaps we can, Mr. Larsen. Perhaps we can."

"Call me, 'Eck.' Just about everyone else does."

"Ok, Let's plan on it, 'Eck.'"

* * * * * *

Just then, Maxine and the others returned in a single vehicle, Castelli's *Mercedes*. Getting out of the car, which they parked off the side of the road, Maxine immediately asked, "Why's that canoe lying down there in the high weeds?"

Joe couldn't resist. "Oh, Eck thought that he was Marlin Perkins on *Wild Kingdom*. Then he found out that a terrified black snake was more than he could handle. Too bad you missed the show. It was a hoot."

"Oh my, Eck, it's such a good thing that you missed out on Vietnam. If you have trouble with Carolina black snakes, how in the world would you deal with Vietnamese pythons?"

"Okay, Max, I've been the butt of enough snake jokes to last me for years. Can we just get this trip moving? It's getting' kind of late isn't it?"

"Yeah, you've got a point there. Sorry it took us so long to get back. The Mercedes came down with a flat tire, and Castelli's spare had its tread partially ripped off. We had to call Triple A to get the tire patched. It ate up a huge chunk of time. So, let's get the life vests on, pack our lunches in the canoes and get this trip launched."

"Sounds good, Max. But can I ask one thing?

"What, Eck?"

"Do you mind carrying your canoe down first?"

* * * * * *

It was nearly 1:15 PM before we pushed off, a full ninety minutes later than Maxine had hoped to get started. But everyone was in high spirits because the day couldn't have been better. The temperature was in the mid-seventies. The sky was a brilliant blue.   And the redbuds and dogwoods were blossoming along the river banks.

As we headed downstream, we encountered lots of canoeists and folks in our party struck up conversations with most of them. When we came upon a troop of Girl Scouts, Olivia became nostalgic and peppered them with questions and advice.

"Hi, girls. You're bringing back such great memories for me. I used to lead canoe trips with the Girl Scouts every summer. My Girl Scout camp was Camp Lou Henry Hoover near the Delaware Water Gap in New Jersey. It is wonderful. If you want to go as a counselor some year get in touch with me at Hillsborough Friends Academy. Just call the school and ask for Olivia. I'll be happy to chat with you, and maybe I can write recommendations for you."

As soon as we were beyond the scouts' hearing range, I had to ask, "Olivia, how do you have even the foggiest notion that any of those girls are people that you would want to write recommendations for."

"I don't."

"Ok, so why'd you offer to write them recommendations?"

"I didn't. You weren't listening very closely, Larsen. I offered to chat with them, and said that ' maybe' I could write recommendations. Probably none of them will call. If any do call, I'll know that they are self-starters and I'll have plenty of opportunity to get a handle on their desire, maturity and capabilities. If the fit is right, I'll write recommendations. If not, I'll find a way to let them down easy. Not-to-worry. I know what I'm doing. I know how to handle teenagers."

"Hey, I wasn't challenging your skill. You're the teen-meister, here. I just wanted to find out how you were going to handle it." I shot back, defensively. She was right. Olivia had a remarkable ability to gauge and manage adolescents. And if we ever had kids of our own, I was glad that she was going to be on my side.

Meanwhile, Vladi and Maxine were quite the pair; splashing each other at regular intervals while belting out Russian and American folk songs. And Vladi appeared totally indifferent to what was developing between Janine and Joe, just two canoes behind him. With the river current flowing slowly and our fleet proceeding at a leisurely pace, Janine took full advantage of the warm sunshine. Moving toward the middle of the canoe and barely paddling at all, she took of her t-shirt, revealing the top of her two-piece swimsuit, and lounged with her back resting on a cushion leaning against the middle thwart. From his seat in the rear of the canoe, Joe, appearing only mildly contorted, extended his right leg forward and massaged Janine's back with his foot, while continuing to paddle for the two of them.

"I've got to hand it to him," I whispered to Olivia. "When he gets locked in on a goal, he won't be denied."

"Yeah, but I hope that he knows where to draw the line in public."

"I think that she'll keep him at bay, at least today. But he seems really interested this time. He'll make his move, for sure."

"What about Vladi?"

"Does it look like he's upset?"

"No. In fact, it looks like he couldn't care less."

"Joe tells me that Janine is just another fling for Vladi; that she knows it; and they're both getting ready to move on."

"And check out Lisa and Jonas over there, Larsen. Compared to Janine and Joe they're the picture of Victorian formality."

"Yeah, well I read Lisa the riot act this morning before we left. I told her that the kid is off limits. She looked at me all shocked, like I'd insulted her. Then she mumbled something about, 'not being someone who robs cradles,' turned around and stormed away from me. But then, she had never seen Jonas before. I think that we still have to keep our eyes on them. She may try to seduce the young stud before the day is over. "

As we talked, Scott and Hilary and Castelli and Suzy propelled their canoes well ahead of the rest of us. Spotting a sand bar, they landed and waved us in for a late lunch. KGB and Rev. Al, bringing up the rear, were the last to beach their canoe. When they arrived, I walked over to them.

"You guys having a good time?"

"Hell, yeah," Al answered. "Old Nikolai here is a natural born river man, and a lot better conversationalist than I'd realized. I think this trip is bringin' him outta his shell."

"I paddle like Al tells me to, and he talks enough for both of us." KGB added in his guttural voice. "But it's fun." He said, flashing a wide grin. "Now, out of my way, Eck. It's time to eat."

Perched on the sandbar, with water flowing around us on both sides, we held a pot-luck picnic.

"Nikolai, I thought you were supposed to bring the barbecue. What's with this three bean salad?" I teased.

"No, no, no I wrote down that I was bringing a salad and hush puppies. You wrote down that you were bringing meat. You should have brought barbeque. This sliced ham is very disappointing, Eck. You owe us all a barbecue dinner."

"Okay, later this spring, we'll dig us a pit behind Carlson and spend a night smokin' a pig the way it's supposed to be done." I offered, surprised how I was warming up to KGB as the day progressed. "Get ahold of yourself, Eck." I thought. "The guy is probably a cold blooded killer. Don't let yourself be fooled."

After we finished eating, we all lounged around on the sandbar for awhile, taking in the sun and watching other canoeists go by. Then, Maxine started shouting out orders.

"It's almost 4:00 and we've only gone about four miles. Everyone, into your canoes.   We've got eight miles to cover before dark. Hop to it."

"What's the problem, Max? The sun won't set until around a quarter to seven? We've already got our meal behind us, and you said that the river is going pick up speed below the bridge." Joe pleaded.

"Yeah, but well before it's dark above the tree line, it's going to be too dark on the river. Actually, I wouldn't be all that concerned if the rest of the trip was like this, all murky and slow, but there are supposed to be some serious rapids on the lower Haw. We gotta be able to see the rocks," Max shot back, urgently.

"You've got a point there," Joe responded getting up, extending a hand to Janine, and moving toward their canoe.

"You mean you've never run this stretch of river before, Maxine?" Olivia quizzed.

"Nope, but I've talked to some folks. There are a few spots where it gets sort of critical."

"A few critical spots," Olivia repeated. "We don't want to be dealing with any critical spots too late in the day. I'm with you. Let's get outta here."

Still, much of our group was slow on the uptake. Vladi had just stretched out face-up in the sand after taking off his t-shirt and khaki shorts, once again revealing the now famous spandex bikini. He flashed Max a look communicating something like, "Are you crazy, Woman, I just got comfortable;" And Suzy, for effect, exaggerating her Long Island accent snapped, "Awww, come awn, Maxeeen. Dis is da best part of da whole trip."

But Max wasn't going to put up with any slackers.

"No back talk, troops. I never should of let us get this far behind. To be safe, we may even have to get out at the bridge. Let's go!"

Seeing that she meant business, we got back into our canoes. Still, our pace hardly met Max's standards. The current wasn't providing much help, and there was a lot of fooling around going on; splashing each other when canoes got close, slowing down while wise-cracks were exchanged and a couple of bathroom stops in the woods.

It was nearly 5:00 when we reached the Haw River Bridge, about midway between Chapel Hill and Pittsboro. We beached in order to talk over our next steps.

Maxine spoke first.

"Okay, Gang. Here's the deal. We've got about an hour and forty-five minutes before sunset. I'm thinking that we should stop here. A couple of us will hitchhike to get my truck and the cars, and we'll come back to pick up the rest of you."

"Come on, Max." Scott shot back. "We haven't seen any rapids all afternoon. We can't bail out now, just when the real fun is going to start."

"Yeah," Castelli chimed in. "It could take a lot longer to hitch to the cars than to paddle to them. After all, they're parked right there at the river. We've already eaten, pooped and peed. The river is going to be running a lot faster. It'll do the work for us. Let's go for it, Max. Let's have some excitement. I'm stoked. How bout you Rev?"

"Max has a damned good point. But the Lord has provided us with a glorious day, and the best stretch of river is ahead of us. I suppose that we can make a go of it, but I don't think we'd better be wastin' any more time. It's now or never, Gang"

No sooner were the words out of Al's mouth than Castelli, with Suzy perched in the front of his canoe, pushed off and started downstream, quickly picking up speed on some small rapids just east of the bridge.

"Yahoo! Let's ride these rapids, you River Rats," Castelli yelled at the top of his lungs.

"Oh, Christ!" Maxine shouted. "The stupid jerk might get us all killed, but we can't let them go alone. Let's go ." Scrambling into our canoes to give chase, we all headed back down the Haw.

* * * * * *

The rapids immediately below the bridge provided the most fun we had experienced all day. After paddling for hours without much help from the river; the additional speed, hearing the clapping of the water over the rocks, and feeling the spray offered a sudden, rejuvenating blast. Joe rose to the occasion by breaking into his John C. Fogerty imitation, singing out Creedence Clearwater Revival's *Proud Mary.*

Left a good job in the city, Working for The Man every night and day, And I never lost one minute of sleeping, Worrying 'bout the way things might have been. Big wheel keep on turning, Proud Mary keep on burning, Rolling, rolling, rolling on the river.

And the rest of us, even KGB, chimed in:

Rolling, rolling, rolling on the river. Rolling, rolling, rolling on the river.

It was great moment, but then the river suddenly slowed down again, and once more, we were paddling hard, trying to maintain some momentum.

"What in the hell happened, Max?" I called out. "I was lookin' forward to some serious whitewater. That was cool, but still pretty tame. Don't ya think?"

"Don't let your briefs get all knotted up, Eck. There are bigger rapids ahead. You'll get your thrill."

Events soon proved her right. After about five minutes of paddling along together, we heard a dull roar coming from somewhere ahead of us. Maxine switched back into her drill sergeant mode, ordering us to pull into a small, protected cove.

"Hear your excitement, Eck? It sounds to me like things are going to be picking up soon, just downstream from here. It's my guess that the river will get critical pretty fast. So, I'm takin' charge. Castelli, if you decide to take off on your own again, I'll track you down and crush your balls. Do you hear me?"

"Aye, aye, Captain," he said, not, for a minute, doubting Maxine.

"Here's the plan. Olivia and Eck, since Olivia has led plenty of canoe trips, you two go first; followed by Castelli and Suzy, Janine and Joe, Scott and Hillary, Vladi and me, and Lisa and Jonas. That will leave Nikolai and the Rev bringing up the rear. Rev., since you have the most white water experience of any of us, I want you in the back in case you have to rescue anyone. Okay?"

"Okay, Max. I've pulled a few from the drink in my time. I figure that I'm still up to it."

"My friends," she warned. " It's already 5:45. We don't have time for foul-ups. Let's push off and get it right the first time."

Once again, we headed down the river, this time with Olivia and me out in front. I was in the rear of the canoe, even though I had offered to move to the front so Olivia, the real canoeist, could steer. But she rejected the plan.

"No, you've been doing fine. I want to be up here spotting rocks. The sun is getting lower and they are going to be hard to see. You listen to me, and head us where I tell you."

I did as I was told, and within a few minutes we began noticeably accelerating. Soon, we were bobbing up and down among sizable waves with impressive rocks all around. For the moment, Olivia was loving it.

"You're doing great, Larsen," she laughed. "Now steer us to the right. We have to get through this shoot. Then take a hard left as soon as we're through. Here we go-o-o!"

I was juiced up and scared as hell. I'd never been on serious rapids before, having only canoed docile sections of the Susquehanna, while in college. It flashed through my mind that, even with all of her Girl Scout river trips, Olivia probably hadn't shot any rapids like these. But I consoled myself.

"What the hell," I thought. "This is what I was hoping for."

Quickly, things began happening far too fast to think about anything except avoiding the rock in front of us; and then missing the next rock, the next, and the next after that. All the while, we were getting drenched by waves slapping up on both sides of the canoe. When we finally popped out into the slower rapids below the treacherous stretch, we were exhilarated, but drained. We paddled over to quiet spot on the side of the river to watch everyone else come through.

I figured that they would be right behind us, but that wasn't the case. Castelli and Suzy got the yips when they watched us, and they pulled over to the other side of the river just before hitting the point of no return. Everyone else pulled over with them. Given the roar of the river, I couldn't tell what orders Maxine was shouting at Castelli, but it was apparent that she was mighty upset. We were losing time, and Maxine was pissed.

After a brief moment of soul searching, Suzy and Castelli mustered up the guts to make a go of it. Everyone else fell into line behind them; spaced just far enough apart to ensure a collision-free passage, if all went well. From where we sat, it was a thing of beauty. Six canoes - two red, one green, two blue, and one yellow - snaking down the river with white water splashing and mist spraying; all against the backdrop of the pine forest with the dimming sun touching the treetops. The paddlers in each canoe whooped it up as they passed through the final critical slot; and upon reaching safety, cheered for those who followed. All the canoes then joined Olivia and me at our quiet pool. Completely stoked, we celebrated our accomplishment.

"Oh, we are so hot!" yelled Joe. "We are so damned hot!"

"Yeah," Hillary chimed in. "We are the badest river team in all the Carolinas. Damn, that was great!"

"Now we've really got something to tell the people back at the dorm," I added.

Glancing around, I saw Vladi, Jonas and KGB, in their separate canoes, in close proximity, bantering away cheerfully. "Who'd have imagined," I thought to myself. "I was worried about KGB snuffing my two guys, and the three of them are having a blast. God only knows what's really going on. I sure can't figure it out."

But Maxine cut the jubilation short, focusing us back to the task at hand.

"Don't pat yourselves on the backs too soon," she warned as she and Vladi circled the rest of us in their canoe. "The toughest part still is ahead."

"What?" Joe shouted, giving voice to what all of us were thinking. "We have to go through something tougher than that?"

"That's what I'm telling you, Darlin.' And like I warned back at the bridge, we're runnin' out of sunlight fast. Let's get movin'. If we get through the next set of rapids, we're home free. We'll still have about a mile and a half to paddle, but it'll be deep and calm with no serious vertical drop. There's a streetlamp nearby the takeout point. It'll shed enough light on the truck and cars, so we can't miss them. Let's go."

"Oh, crap," I thought. "Darkness is gonna be a problem. Clouds are moving in, blocking what's left of the sun. It'll be dusk in no time"

"Will you be able to spot the rocks, okay?" I asked Olivia, as we broke out of the pack. Paddling quickly down river.

"I'm not sure. I had some trouble back at the last chute. I

guess we'll find out, won't we."

"Guess so."

After about ten minutes, the river began picking up speed, again. As we started sliding down the rapids, in the same order that Maxine had previously dictated, I began worrying that things might spiral out of control. I wasn't so worried about Olivia and me, because Olivia was really damned good at this. But what about the others?

Suddenly, we began moving much faster. The approaching rocks didn't appear any larger or more dangerous than those we had already conquered, but it looked like the overall run might be quite a bit longer. Then, as we entered the whitewater, Olivia cried out.

"Larsen, there's not enough light. The shadows are gone ! Unless they're sticking out way above the surface, I can't see the rocks in front of us."

"We'll be okay, " I shouted. "We'll be okay."

No sooner were the words out of my mouth than we hit a rock head on. Olivia flipped forward, falling head-over-heals out of the front of the canoe. In a flash, I passed her by, as she was flailing in the water.

"Olivia , Olivia," I screamed, glancing back at her. Seeing a little pool to my left, I desperately steered the canoe towards it, and jumped out, landing on my feet in water about chest deep, beyond the rip of the whitewater. As Olivia swept by I frantically extended my paddle to her. Somehow, she grabbed it and held on, and I pulled her towards me.

"Christ, are you alright?"

"Soaked, cold…" she sputtered. "I hit my head pretty hard on a rock, but I didn't swallow any water. Thank God for this life jacket. This is why I always tell you to wear a life jacket, Larsen."

"I get your point, Honey. And I'm glad to see that you're making the most of a teachable moment."

There was still enough light for me to see blood oozing from a gash at the front of Olivia's temple. I pulled out a wet bandana from my back pocket and handed it to her.

"Here, hold this up against the cut on your head and keep hanging on to the canoe. I've got to warn the rest not to hit the rock that did us in."

But it was too late to warn anybody about anything. Others were already nearly on top of us. Within moments, chaos reigned.

Suzy and Castelli, following directly behind us, somehow missed the rock, only to capsize about 15 yards further downstream. Their canoe flipped and both landed in the river, floundering around in the boiling water as their canoe washed downstream. Meanwhile, Janine and Joe, following too closely, came barreling by, with Joe again bellowing, " *Rolling, Yeah, Rolling, Rolling on the river.*" The stern of their canoe barely missed Castelli's head; but fortunately, both Suzy and Castelli recovered. Swept downstream, they slowly made their way to the river bank about fifty yards below Olivia and me.

"Damn, that was close," I yelled to Olivia. "But I think Joe and Janine are going to make it." And they did, speeding far down the river without capsizing. The same was true for Scott and Hillary, descending virtually the exact same path as Joe and Janine.

"Okay," I wondered. "So far half of us have ditched and half have made it through. Who's next?"

No sooner did I finish the thought then along came the three remaining canoes, closely packed together, careening down the river. Maxine, seeing Olivia and me in distress steered hard in our direction, trying to come to our aid. But Vladi, in her bow, failed to spot a submerged boulder. Taking a direct hit, Vladi, still in his bikini and a life vest, flew into the air, landing outside of the canoe and smashing his shoulder on yet another rock. Although clearly hurt, he managed to cling to the rock with his uninjured arm. Meanwhile, Maxine stayed put in the rear, but the canoe did a 180 degree spin, heading backwards downstream. She missed colliding with any further rocks, skirting several dangerous spots before righting herself downriver, almost out of our sight.

In hot pursuit, Lisa and Jonas followed next. Missing the rocks that had scuttled us, Jonas masterfully steered the canoe into the safe harbor sheltering Olivia and me. Upon arriving, Jonas dove out of the canoe, swimming against the raging current towards Vladi.

Before he could get there, KGB and Rev. Al's onrushing canoe struck him in the head.

"Christ," I yelled, "You're going to kill him." As the words spilled out of my mouth, a thought flashed through my mind, "But that's what you were sent to do, you Son of a Bitch! You're just gonna make it look like an accident."

His head still above water, Vladi struggled to hold on to the rock with his one good arm. With, KGB and Rev. Al just beyond us, paddling hard to get to shore, and Jonas appearing lifeless in the water; I sprang into action. Diving into the current, I swam at an angle giving me a decent shot of intercepting Jonas as he was dragged down the river. Within a few seconds, I made contact, and wrapped my arm around his shoulder. Struggling to keep his head above water, I swam, as best I could, toward the riverbank.

But I wasn't strong enough. The current swept us away, pulling us both under.

"Damn it," I cried to myself. "We're going down for good."

Later, Olivia told me that she let out a horrendous scream. But I couldn't hear anything but the roar of the river as our entangled bodies were pulled to the bottom.

Then, out of nowhere, a third body appeared. A strong

arm encircled me, a big hand grabbed ahold of Jonas' shirt, and we were yanked upwards. As my head cleared the surface, I recognized KGB, dragging us across the current to within a few feet of a paddle extended by Rev. Al, who was squatting on a rock. In one swift motion, KGB latched onto the paddle and Al pulled us in. Seeing that I was conscious, Al immediately performed CPR on Jonas, who miraculously had not drowned and was soon spitting up water and breathing on his own.

KGB didn't linger to watch any of this. In a flash, he darted over several rocks to the river bank, ran upstream and leaped into the river, letting the current take him to Vladi. The next thing that I could see was both of them perched on the rock with KGB barking orders.

Realizing that KGB was his only hope, the badly injured poet wrapped his one good arm around his countryman's waist, and the two of them crashed into the water. Valiantly, KGB struggled against the current trying to haul his massive load to safety, but the two were soon smashing against rocks, while being swept downstream.

Seeing the nightmare unfolding, Rev. Al handed Jonas' over to Olivia, who had joined us on our safe perch. Al, paddle in hand, skipped from boulder to boulder, somehow maintaining his footing on the slick, spray-covered surfaces. His one hope was to intercept them at a precipice, jutting into the river immediately before a steep drop-off into a swirling basin. Al reached his target just before the Russians came hurdling through. Lying on his stomach and leaning as far out into the river as he could, he extended the paddle into the river.

As the Russians came by, KGB flipped Vladi towards Al, so the poet could grab the paddle with his one good arm. But in doing so, the spy eliminated any possibility that he, too, could grasp the paddle. As Vladi lunged, locking onto the paddle, KGB released him, to avoid pulling both Vladi and Al into the water; and by doing so, he sacrificed himself to the river. Al last saw KGB as he descended, head-first into the raging basin.

"Oh, My God!" I screamed. "He didn't make it. He saved us all, and he didn't make it".

I cried like a baby over the man I'd been cursing just a few minutes before.

* * * * * *

We all needed time to deal with the shock of everything that had transpired, but we didn't have the luxury. It was almost dark. We could barely see the rocks well enough to make our way to shore. Jonas was terribly weak, but pushed on; his youth and incredible vitality serving him well. Vladi, in severe pain but still ambulatory, followed Jonas to shore. Olivia, having stemmed the bleeding from her head wound, scrambled behind Vladi. I, pretty much recovered from my dunking, followed behind her. Al, still riding the adrenaline surge of his rescue efforts, brought up the rear, ready to take charge when we reached the river's edge.

Suzy and Castelli, wet and shaken, had successfully crawled ashore downstream and walked along the river bank to meet us. Meanwhile, Maxine, Joe, Janine and Hillary and Scott had all been whisked so far downstream that they had no choice but to continue on, uncertain about what had happened to us.

We gathered our three remaining canoes – Suzy's and Castelli's was swept down river when they capsized - and beached them, nearby. For a few brief moments, we sat in the dark trying to come to grips with what we had gone through.

" How ya doin,' Jonas?" Olivia asked.

"Better than I was, but not too good," Jonas muttered.

"Thank God, you're alive. And you, Vladi?"

Vladi really wasn't up to answering questions in his limited

English, so Jonas, whose second language was Russian, translated for him.

"He says that his shoulder feels like it has a red hot poker stuck in it, but that he's known worse pain. He can move on."

Al spoke up above the chatter.

"Okay, Folks, we gotta haul ass outta here. There's a road that parallels the river, not too far away. I guess it's no more than a quarter mile. Once we reach it, the road will take us to our cars. We just have to make our way through this here underbrush and woods to reach it. My hunch is that if we stay headed perpendicular to the river, we'll run into a path sometime soon. But it would sure as hell be a lot easier if we could see more than a few feet in front of us!"

Al was right. We had no flashlights and there was no moonlight. Even if the moon had been out, the tree canopy was sufficiently thick that it probably wouldn't have done us much good. The visibility was so bad that we had to get down on our hands and knees to feel our way along. But first, Rev Al insisted on offering up a prayer for KGB.

"Dear Heavenly One, we pray for the spirit of our departed comrade, Nikolai. May his journey to the other side be peaceful and guided by all of the good karma that he accumulated in these last hours of his life. May it serve him well during whatever lies ahead. We badly misjudged him, Great One, and we're saddened that we didn't really get to know the heroic soul that we met today. May we all lead better lives, inspired by his example. Amen."

Like the rest of the crew, I chimed in "Amen." But then an idea hit me.

"Uh, Al?"

"Yeah, Eck."

"We don't really know if KGB is dead or alive. I mean stranger things have happened."

"You're right, Eck. We don't know and stranger things have happened. But I'd wager much of what I own on his time bein' up. You didn't see what I saw. Below me, out there, the water was crashing on rocks. I saw his head hit one and bounce onto another before he was swept into a deep hole. And he didn't pop up again. The gig is over for KGB."

Unable to refute Al's logic, I tried to put the tragedy behind me and focus on getting out to the road.

Tapped by Al to lead the way, I got down on my hands and knees and began moving forward in the dark tangle of underbrush between the edge of the river and the surrounding forest. Olivia followed behind me with the rest of our crew – single file – behind her, moving slowly at a right angle from the river. Assuming that I was doomed to picking up dozens of ticks, I worked at making plenty of noise to scare away any snakes that might be in our path.

"Larsen?"

"What, Olivia?"

"Do you have to snort and growl? It's getting on my nerves."

"I'm just trying to make sure that no copperhead or rattler gets you, Honey."

"Trust me, Larsen. Snakes don't hear sounds like we do. They pick up vibrations from the ground. Any snakes in front of us are getting out of the way of this thundering herd. They don't want to be dealing with us anymore than we want to be dealing with them. So, settle down and keep moving forward. You're safe."

"Yes, Dear." I responded, humiliated by my second snake snafu of the day.

But as it turned out, Vladi – responding to intense pain - soon began making enough noise to scare away any wildlife within miles. Following behind Olivia, he let out loud groans every 20 yards or so, and periodically pounded the ground with his fist to vent his frustration. His shoulder had to be throbbing, but the histrionics seemed over-the-top; especially in contrast with Jonas, who, in spite of a likely concussion and near drowning, quietly crawled along behind the wounded Russian bear.

Above the din, Al called out to me from the rear of the pack.

"Hey, Eck, any sign of a break ahead?"

"Christ, Al, I can't even see the bushes we're crawling through. I can only feel them in front of me. To tell you the truth it doesn't feel any different than it did 20 minutes ago, just a lot of stickers scratching the hell out of me and Kudzu vines hopelessly tangled up with each other. Why don't we trade places and let you try bulldozing your way through this crap?"

Then, just as I finished my grousing, my hands, and then my head, popped through the thicket into a clearing. I crawled all the way out and discovered that we had come upon the path that Al had predicted we'd find.

"Oh, yeah, Baby. We found it. Here's the path. Push on through folks. We found the freakin' path."

The whole crew whooped it up. And within a few minutes we were all standing huddled together.

"Ok, Al. Where do we go now?" Olivia asked.

"I don't know."

"What do yo mean, 'You don't know'?" She shot back.

"Just like I said. 'I don't know.' Hell, I've never been here before and I'm just like you. I can't see my hand in front of my face. Maybe we should go upstream, or maybe we should go down. It all depends where the path veers closest to the road. It's a coin toss. Your call. But whatever way we go, we're still gonna have to get back down on our hands and knees to feel our way along. Otherwise, we're going to keep stumblin' back into the brush, or hitin'our heads on low-hanging branches."

On that cheery note, Olivia opted for, "Downstream." And we all got back down on all fours, with me again leading the way. We plodded forward for what seemed like an hour when Olivia called out, "Did you hear that, Larsen?"

"What?"

"It's a car, or a truck, not too far off to our left."

"Sorry, I don't hear a thing. We just gotta keep moving"

"Hey, I heard it." Castelli chimed in. "And I glimpsed a headlight. Hang a left, Eck, the road is just off to our left."

I did as I was told, and within a few minutes we were all standing on a dark country road. The car that Castelli spotted was long gone, but at least we were out of the woods, knowing that our cars were parked just a few miles away.

Hoping to avoid a time-consuming caravan, I offered to run ahead.

"Hey, I'm the only runner here. I'm going to take off down the road. Hopefully, Joe and the others are waiting there and we'll be able to come back and get everyone in one trip."

"Larsen, don't leave. This has been hard enough already. I don't want to get separated now that it looks like we're safe." Olivia pleaded.

"Yeah. I know, Olivia. But everyone's exhausted. It's getting colder out. We've got to get warm and dry as soon as we can. It's probably no more than three miles to the cars. I know that I can be there in a less than twenty-five minutes, and get right back here. It's going to take over twice that long with us all dragging along, and I don't think that Vladi is even up to it.

"Why don't we hitch hike?"

"Would you stop on a dark road in the middle of nowhere to pick up a group of strangers? If you get a ride, you can stop and pick me up along the way. In the meantime, I'm taking off. Come on, give me a kiss."

Reluctantly, she did. And off I went, running directly down the middle of the road, in order to avoid twisting an ankle on the uneven shoulder. Unfortunately, I hadn't counted on the river sand in my old, soaked running shoes.

"Oh God, I'm gonna have the worst blisters of my entire life! But I've gotta push through it."

So I trotted along, with each step an irritating reminder of the bloodied feet that awaited me. After roughly a mile, I still hadn't seen any cars. Then, off in the distance heading towards me, there was the single headlight of a motorcycle, moving at a pretty good clip.

"Hey, help is on the way." I whispered to myself. "I hope this guy stops."

I stood my ground in the middle of the road, waving my arms wildly, trying to look as distressed as I possibly could. Soon the cyclist was upon me, so much so that I nearly got hit. He cursed me as he flew by.

"Holy shit, that was close." I thought, catching my breath and stumbling forward. Then, behind me, there was the screeching sound of the motorcyclist hitting his breaks, going into a sideways slide and coming to a halt. In a heartbeat, he was rumbling towards me again. The chopper immediately caught up to me, repeated the same slamming on the breaks routine, slid past me on the right, and came to a halt about ten feet in front of me.

"What in the hell you trying to do, Buddy, get yourself killed? You're damned lucky I didn't split you right down the middle."

The words were tough, but as they assaulted me, I realized that the person behind the headlight hardly looked intimidating at all. Dressed in black leather and helmetless, the rider sitting astride the bike was short, maybe 5 feet tall. And *he* wasn't a *he* at all; but a woman with spiked, crew-cut hair.

Having been through so much in the previous few hours, the last thing in the world that I wanted to do was get into an argument with anyone, much less some woman biker dude. But, a torrent of words came tumbling out, as I fought back tears.

"Look, Mister or Sister, or whatever you are, I already was nearly killed on the river, along with half the people in my group. We lost one guy, and I'm pretty damned upset about it; so I don't need to be putting up with any shit from you or anyone else. Can you give me a ride a few miles down the road, to my car, or are you going to be one more screw-up in the worst day of my life?"

"Hey Buddy, calm down, calm down. I didn't know that you'd been shipwrecked on the Haw. I'll give you a ride. Hop on the back. How far down the road? "

It was a good question, because I really didn't know for sure how far down the road we had to go.

"I don't know for sure. We've got a car and a truck parked at the take out point about 6 miles below the Pittsboro Road. Do you know that spot?"

"Yeah, I know the place. I've had some good times there. Me and my friends float the river in tubes now and then and party there when we get out. But we never shoot the spring, heavy rapids. Even late in the summer, when the river is runnin' low, we hop out and carry the tubes past the big boulders. So, you guys tried shootin' the Haw's killer rapids?"

"Yeah."

"Well, congratulations on survivin'. You must be one tough mother."

"Never particularly thought of myself as tough, but maybe so."

"Or maybe you're just damned lucky."

"That's probably more likely the case."

"So, what's your name lucky man?"

"Eckhardt Larsen. You can call me Eck. Yours?"

"Shane Long. People call me Long Shane. Sarcasm, you know. You can call me Shane, or Long or Long Shane. Whatever's your preference.".

"Good meeting you, Long One. Let's get rolling." I said while slipping onto the back of her Harley. "I gotta get back and pick up my friends."

"Okay. Were outta here."

In less than five minutes we arrived at our destination. Of the three vehicles we had parked at the take out point, only the truck remained, and the only member of our party in sight was Joe. As we pulled up, he greeted me with a barrage of comments and questions.

"Well if it isn't the Big Guy, himself. I see you got yourself a new girlfriend. Olivia give up on you after you threw her out of the canoe? Nice cycle. Where's everyone else? What happened to them? Did ya notice that I did so much better than you at shooting rapids? Want to go back and try it again? You actually had me worried. What are we gonna do now?"

"Oh, Christ would you shut up, and pay my driver for me. I lost my wallet on the river."

"No need, Eck. The taxi service is on me."

"Thanks, Shane. Maybe I can repay the favor sometime."

"Hope not, Buddy. Have yourself a good life. I'm late for a party."

"Hey, can you do one more thing?" I asked.

"What's that?"

"When you pass our friends on the road, will you let them know that we're on our way to pick them up?"

"Sure, no problema Eck. Consider it done."

And she revved up her machine and took off down the road.

"So, the first answer is, No." I sputtered to Joe.

"No to what."

"No, I don't want to go back and do it again. It was a damned catastrophe. Have you seen KGB? Did he wash up downstream?"

"Wash up? What do ya mean, 'Wash up?'"

" I mean KGB drowned. He's dead. The guy saved me, Jonas and Vladi. Then he drowned. He was a hero, but then he got swept under." I choked up, unsuccessfully holding back my tears.

"Jesus, I...I had no idea."

"Of course not, I was just hoping that maybe we could recover his body. God knows where he is. He could be lodged between logs or rocks somewhere upstream. He may have floated by. It's so damned dark out there. Who knows? Who knows? We gotta move on. The rest of the group is about three miles up the road. Let's go pick them up. Christ, I'm exhausted. You take control, ok?"

"Yeah, yeah, yeah. Don't worry. We've only got the truck, but we can fit everyone in the cab and the bed. Maxine, Hillary and Scott already went back to the dorm to get help and report to the police that we might need a rescue team. Anyway, Eck, it's good to see you in one piece. Can I give you a big, wet kiss?"

"I appreciate the sentiment, but spare me the agony of slobbering all over me. Can we just get going?"

"Yeah, sure. Jump in the cab. There's a blanket in there to help you warm up. "Let's get everyone else, and head straight to the dorm. Some of us can come back tomorrow, find the canoes and get the cars that are upriver."

As we approached the truck, I saw that Janine was inside, waking up, stretching and wiping the sleep from her eyes.

"Eck, thank God you're here." She exclaimed as Joe opened the cab door. "Where's Vladi? Where is everyone else? What happened to you all? "

I gave Janine a hug and settled down next to her, while Joe climbed into the driver's seat. As we headed down the road, I filled her in, as best I could, on all that had happened; assuring her that Vladi was ok, though beaten up. When I finished my account, I noticed that we'd seemed to have overshot our destination.

"Whoa, Joe. We've gone too far. Didn't you see everyone on the side of the road?"

"Nope. I didn't see anybody. Did you?"

"Ah, no. I didn't. I didn't see anyone at all. They should have been huddled up there on the left, a little ways back. Quick, let's turn around."

So, Joe came to a halt, made a U-turn, and we headed back.

"Stop, stop right here. This is where we came out of the woods. I recognize that telephone pole with the Jesse Helms sticker on it. Damn it. I don't need this. What else can go wrong? Where in the hell are they?"

"Easy, Eck, easy. We'll find them." Joe cooed, sounding uncharacteristically calm and reassuring.

"Fine, fine. But don't patronize me, Chin Man. I'm freakin' fallin' apart, and you owe it to me to fall apart with me. I need company, right now. I need you to panic right along with me. Do you hear me?"

"Geez, you are messed up. I hear you, but I'm not so sure that's what we need right now......Hey, look. There's a light in the woods up to the left. It looks like there's a house back there. I'll turn down the driveway to see if that's where they are."

"Ok. Do whatever you want to do. Just make things right. It's time for things to turn out right. I'm holding you responsible. Understand?"

"No problem. 'Right' is my middle name. I guarantee things will be alright."

The dirt driveway was badly rutted, just like you might

expect in the back woods of North Carolina. As we approached the modest frame house, two chained-up rottweilers began barking and a flood-lamp switched on, filling the front yard with light. We pulled closer to the house and a fifty-something, weather-beaten woman came out the front door and approached us. Not bothering to exchange pleasantries, she launched into a scolding monologue.

"They're all inside tryin' to warm up. I'm getting' a little soup in em. I called the county sheriff and they're sendin' the rescue squad over to take the big Russian and the young fella to the hospital in Chapel Hill to get em checked out. I been tellin' em that they're damned lucky to be alive. That stretch of river will claim ya this time of year. It's always the damned fool college kids that try to run it in the spring. We lost two last year. Now, it sounds like we've lost another. Come on in, and make sure to wipe your feet on the rug by the door. I'm Martha Mebane. Who are you?"

We shared our names as we walked towards the door. When we entered Martha's big country kitchen, everyone was sitting around the oversized table exhausted and pretty well beaten up. Olivia jumped up and gave us all hugs, but the best any of the others could do was crack a weak smile.

But Joe was undaunted.

"Not-to-worry everyone," he proclaimed. "The rescue team is here. Eck has charged me with making everything 'right' and I'm up to the task."

His timing was impeccable. No sooner were the words out of his mouth than three county sheriff's cars and the rescue squad ambulance pulled into the driveway. Within minutes, Vladi and Jonas were off to the hospital. Rev. Al gave a statement to an officer, who indicated that the search for KGB's body would begin at dawn. The officer then asked if we wanted to go back up river to collect our remaining cars, or return to the dorm. Everyone opted for Carlson. The cars and canoes could wait until tomorrow.

Castelli, Suzy, Al and Lisa piled into a patrol car, which quickly headed off to Chapel Hill. Joe, Janine, Olivia and I lagged behind to thank Martha for her help. Then we squeezed into the cab of Maxine's truck and headed home. On arriving in Chapel Hill, we wanted to check on Vladi and Jonas. Since the dorm was close to the medical center, we parked at Carlson and made the short walk up the hill to North Carolina Memorial Hospital. By the time we got to there, it was almost midnight. A man at the information desk called the nursing station on Vladi's and Jonas' floor and found out that neither was in any real danger, but they both were being held overnight for observation. Assured that they were resting comfortably, and told that we would not be able to see either of them until noon on Sunday, we headed back to the dorm.

Strolling down the hill on what, in spite of the hellacious day, was now a beautiful evening, I said to Olivia. "So, let's get right in your car and head over to Hillsborough."

"Larsen," she responded looking at me sweetly, but exhaustedly. "I'll cave in on staying at the dorm. I can't see going all the way to Hillsborough, only to have to get up and come back in the morning to check on Jonas. Let's sleep in your room tonight."

"My room. We're going to break the taboo and stay in my room! Maybe this hasn't been such a bad day after all."

"To sleep, Larsen, only to sleep."

"Not-to-worry, My Love. Sleep is about all I have left in me, tonight."

Reaching Carlson, the four of us entered the deserted lobby and walked to the elevator. When we got in, Joe hit the 3rd floor button, for his room, and the 4th floor button for the Janine's (and Vladi's) room, as well as mine. None of us spoke on the elevator, as we were all running on fumes. Then, when the door opened on the 3rd floor, both Joe and Janine stepped out and headed towards Joe's room. It hadn't occurred to me, until that moment, that they were spending the night together.

As they glided away, Joe glanced back over his shoulder, flashed a sarcastic grin and said, "Good night, you two. Enjoy your good night's sleep."

Chapter 8
Farewells

On Sunday morning, as we were headed out for breakfast, Olivia and I bumped into Wolf in the Carlson lobby

"Hey, Wolfie. How you doing? Did you hear about KGB?" I asked.

"Castelli filled me in when the sheriff brought him home, last night. It's too bad."

"He died a hero. I'd have probably drowned, if not for him."

"I guess you can never tell. And did you hear our news?"

"What's that?"

"We broke the code on the wiretap tapes?"

"You did? What did you and Charlotte find out?"

"Well, it wasn't really us. Moe broke the code."

"Moe! Why'd you give him the tapes? Why'd you let him know that you were doing something illegal?" I asked incredulously, not letting on that I had alerted Moe to the wiretapping the night before the canoe trip.

"We were stumped, Eck. We were gettin' nowhere, and he's freakin' brilliant. Somehow, he'd already figured out that we'd been tapping KGB's phone. I don't know how he did it, but he figured it out; and he flat out asked me if I needed help decipherin' the code? So, with him already knowin' it was a no-brainer. Make sense now?"

"Yeah, it does. So what did Moe find out?"

"Turns out, it wasn't such a dangerous situation after all. I'd never have guessed it, but in the final tape KGB pretty much told his boss at the KGB to kiss off. He told him that he'd had enough of spying and that he was going to start life over, stay in grad school, and making a fresh start in the Land of the Free and the Home of the Brave."

"Oh, Christ, what a tragedy. Did you have to tell me that, Wolfman?"

"But you asked, Eck."

"You did ask, Larsen." Olivia chimed in. " At least now we really know what kind of man saved your life, and that he spent his last few days as a free man. Doesn't that make you feel any better?"

"I suppose so."

"There's more," Wolf added.

"What else?" I asked.

"The spook in Moscow told KGB that if he was serious about bailing out on them, he might as well consider himself to be a dead man. KGB knew what they are capable of doing. He must have realized that he was living on borrowed time."

"Well, at the end he certainly acted like a man who had nothing to lose. It's crazy how things work out sometimes. But life goes on, I guess. Listen, we're going to grab a bite to eat then get ourselves over to the hospital to check on Vladi and Jonas. If you run into Joe and Janine, tell them that we'll see them there."

"Sure."

"Thanks, Wolfman. And thanks for solving the KGB mystery for us."

"Think nothin' of it, Eck. Be sure to thank Moe when you see him."

It was another brilliant day, and Olivia and I enjoyed our

leisurely walk across campus to Franklin Street, where we purchased coffee and bagels, before heading to the hospital. The previous evening, just before falling into a deep sleep, Olivia contacted Jonas' host family, alerting them to his hospitalization and assuring them that she would closely monitor the situation and return Jonas home on Sunday, after his physicians released him. Following the hospital visit, I planned on heading back to the river with Joe, Maxine and a few others to pick up the canoes and cars.

Approaching the hospital, we spotted Janine and Joe about fifty yards ahead of us, at the main entrance.

"They're holding hands!" I exclaimed.

"Is that such a big surprise, after they slept together last night?"

"But how are they going to this finesse this with Vladi?"

"Weren't you just telling me, yesterday, that she knew it was pretty much over between them?"

"Yeah, I did; but Joe predicted this all the first time that he saw her. How could he have known? I mean we're talking Joe, of all people."

"Larsen, has it ever occurred to you that you underestimate him?"

"Nope, that has never occurred to me."

"Well, maybe it should."

Realizing I was sounding like a dunce, I stifled any further remarks and demurely accompanied Olivia into the hospital and up to Vladi's and Jonas' floor. We arrived at Vladi's room first.

As we entered, Janine and Joe were standing at the foot of the hospital bed. And much to our surprise, Wilma, the lecherous law student who had been lusting after Vladi since day one, was sitting next to Vladi, holding his hand.

"Oh my God," I thought. "We've entered the *Twilight Zone*." Then, I sputtered, "Vladi, how ya feelin', Buddy?" and

"Wilma, so great of you to be here to check on our man."

"Been here since 3:00 AM, Eck."

"But there were no visitors allowed. They kicked us out last night."

"You've got to work the system, Eck. I know a few nurses up here on the floor. And I knew that Vladi was gonna be needin' some female comfortin'." She said, shooting a disdainful glance at Janine. "Everything is under control here. Why don't you all go check on Jonas. The boy hasn't had anyone in to see him yet."

Janine appeared perfectly comfortable with Wilma's suggestion; or more accurately, her order. But before turning and leading the way out of the room, she put her hand on Vladi's foot, calmly saying a few sentences to him in Russian. Vladi, still obviously in pain, gave a wry smile and nodded his head.

Joe and Janine headed out of the room, with Olivia and me following. In the hallway, Olivia caught up with Janine and Joe fell back next to me. As we headed toward Jonas' room, I whispered to Joe, "What in the hell is going on? Have I been living on a different planet or something?"

"Maybe," Joe shot back. "You've got that alien quality about you; bulbous head, green complexion."

"Ok, Smart Ass, good line. But what's happening here?"

"Janine told me, yesterday, that Vladi's been sneaking some on the side with Wilma for the last several weeks. I told you things were winding down between the two of them. I think that Vladi must have picked up on the fact that destiny had delivered Janine to a superior specimen, the man of her dreams; and he decided to move on to greener pastures. She just told him that it was over between them, and she wished him well. She also told him not to hurt himself, cause Wilma can get pretty rough."

"How do you know? She was speaking in Russian."

"Well, she told me last night, in bed, that she was planning on ending it with Vladi, today. And I just made up the part about Wilma."

With Olivia's scolding still ringing in my ears, I spit out the words I thought that I would never utter.

"Congratulations, Joe. It's clear that I've really underestimated you."

"Could I hear that one more time, please?"

"No, I've said it once. That's gonna have to do."

"I'll always remember this moment, Eck.'

"Yeah, me too."

We caught up to Olivia and Janine outside of Jonas' doorway. Entering, we found two young, attractive nurses tending to a smiling Jonas, who appeared free of any physical discomfort. The nurses were briefing him for his discharge and, as we later discovered, exchanging telephone numbers with him. His doctors wanted Jonas to go home to Hillsborough to rest for 48 hours. So, I hustled back to Carlson to get Olivia's car, while everyone else stayed and visited. When I returned, Jonas was showered and ready to go.

Olivia took Jonas to Hillsborough, while Joe and Janine - now appearing inseparable - and I went back to Carlson to connect with Maxine, in order to collect the canoes and cars. As we stood in the parking lot waiting to depart, Joe delivered a shot.

"Another beautiful, North Carolina day, Eck. Why don't you and I grab two canoes and do it all again. I'll teach you how to tame the mighty Haw."

"And how about if I just strangle you right here?"

"Oh, guess I hit a sore spot. Sorry, Big Guy."

* * * * * *

By supper, we returned and were all filing back into the dorm. As we entered the lobby, Moe was standing at the desk talking to Suzy. He leaned over the counter, kissed her and came to greet us.

"I understand you had quite the harrowing experience, my friends."

"More harrowing for some than for others," Joe added. "But if you include being worried sick about those who fell into the drink, it was pretty rough all the way around."

"And I understand that Mr. Andropov paid the ultimate price, dying a hero's death."

"He saved my life, Moe; and Jonas' and Vladi's as well. Who'd have thought it?"

"Spies are very unusual people, Eckhardt. They lead lives of deception; but they are very talented and can be very honorable people, if they are on your side."

While listening, I realized that Moe could just as easily be talking about himself as about KGB. He continued.

"I suppose that my work here is complete."

"I don't think so, Moe," I said, realizing I didn't want him to leave "They haven't found KGB's body yet. You'd better stick around."

"What's the purpose? He saved the lives of the people that I was here to protect. If he reappears, he's no threat. In fact, if he reappears, more power to him. I wish him a long and prosperous life. Besides, I have some pressing business to attend to up north. I have to be on my way. It has been splendid getting to know you all, but it is time to move on. Please give my warm wishes to your lovely Olivia. Tell her I regret not having the opportunity to say farewell in person."

With that, he gave me and Joe firm handshakes, and Janine a hug and a kiss on the cheek. He turned, headed through the lobby doors, and ambled off towards the Carolina Inn.

"Damn it, I didn't remember to thank him for breaking the code. I wanted to hear about that, and there was so much more that I wanted to talk to him about," I murmured, saddened and shaken by Moe's departure. "He's a goldmine of information. I was really growing fond of him."

Janine chimed in, "He's a fascinating character, Eck, but not cut out for long-term relationships. Grass doesn't grow under Moe Berg's feet."

"I guess not. I'll just have to track him down some day and take him out for a reunion lunch. You know Moe. He won't pass up free food and an opportunity to spin tales about old times."

* * * * * *

The month leading up to graduation flew by. People in Carlson hit the books extra hard; even Joe, who under Janine's influence began showing uncharacteristically studious behavior. I was swamped; wrapping up internship projects for the radio station, studying for comprehensive exams and putting the finishing touches on my thesis on the history of radio sports coverage. And even though HFA's school year ended a month after UNC's, Olivia's work also picked up dramatically, as she coached spring lacrosse and gave extra time to graduating students working on their senior projects.

With all of the emotional turmoil immediately following the river trip and the flood of work during the push to graduation, Joe's and my job searches fell through the cracks. A few nights before the commencement ceremony, with our parents already headed south to see us graduate, the two of us went to the Carolina Coffee Shop for a late dinner. Sitting in a booth, we wrestled with the situation.

"Looks like we kind of dropped the ball on the job front," I offered.

"Yeah, but it could have been worse."

"How, so? I think we put out a total of about three applications each, and neither of us got an interview."

"Think positively, Eck. We could have flunked out of school, but we didn't. In fact we both did pretty damned well, even me. I'm getting a 3.8 this semester. I'm finally getting the hang of this."

"Nice glass half-full approach. But let's focus on the future. We've got to come up with some options."

" We can always return to Ocean City and work on the boardwalk."

"And live at home to save some money."

"Yeah, and surf every morning, play tennis in the afternoon, and go to the bars at night."

"A return to our teenage years, it's got its merits, but we'd be going backwards. What about the women in our lives? And we have master's degrees. Shouldn't we finally be mastering something beyond what we did in high school?"

"Ok, Eck. Scratch returning to the womb. What else? Well, we can always enlist."

"We're against the war, remember?"

"Ok, how about the Peace Corps?"

"Not a bad idea. We'll go abroad for a couple of years, dragging Olivia and Janine along with us, hone our foreign language skills, and do good deeds while working for peanuts. I'll run a 50 watt radio station in a Guatemalan jungle, and you can do community development work jump starting a tennis or soccer program for nomad kids living on the edge of the Sahara. I'll get malaria and you'll probably get bitten by a puff adder, but we'll make a real contribution to humanity. I only see one glitch in the whole plan."

"Enlighten me?"

"Olivia won't want to leave her job, and I'm not trekking halfway around the globe without her."

"Sounds like you're locking yourself into a 30 mile radius of Chapel Hill, Big Guy."

"Seems that way, but the Peace Corps is still an option for you."

"Probably not."

"How come?"

"Last night I murmured something to Janine about never wanting to leave her, and there's no way that she is going to drop out of her post-doc program."

"Did I hear you correctly? Did you say, 'Never wanting to leave her.'"

"That's what you heard."

"But surely you've used that line before."

"Maybe once or twice, but this time I meant it."

"So, it looks like we're in the same boat."

"A slow boat to nowhere."

But in that instant, I envisioned a solution.

"Problem solved," I said, visibly perking up.

"How so? Stay in Chapel Hill and wait tables?"

"Maybe some of that along the way, but think again. It is so damned obvious."

Joe pondered his answer. Then a sly grin came across his face. "Are you thinking what I think you're thinking?"

"Yeah, Man. Question: Why did they put Blue Heaven here in the first place? Answer: For folks like us to keep collecting degrees."

"Doctoral programs!" We both shouted, simultaneously jumping up and giving each other a high five.

And so, we both set about trying to get back into graduate school.

* * * * * *

A few days after graduation, Carlson was pretty much cleared out. Some students, including Vladi, had moved to apartments in Chapel Hill or Carrboro. Others had simply headed home. Most of the staff was ready to go, too. A few would remain as a skeleton crew during summer school, but most had either graduated or were moving to apartments. Of course, Wolf would stay on; but of the remaining R.A.'s, only Charlotte was signing up for another full year. Even Rev. Al had decided to change course by moving to a house in the country. A new R.D. was scheduled to arrive June 1st.

But before anyone departed, the Rev. decided to have a staff farewell blow-out. Doing it up right, we strung lanterns around the volleyball court; brought in a couple of kegs; ordered barbecue, slaw and hush puppies from Allen and Son's; put the dorm's big speakers outside; and let loose one last time.

I was in pretty good spirits because Olivia came for the occasion, promising to spend the night. But throughout the evening, there was an undertone of regret. We'd gone through a lot together over the course of two years, and now our little family was breaking up. Close to midnight, with us all overstuffed and a little drunk, the party began winding down and the goodbyes began in earnest.

"Hey, it's been great." I more or less repeated, over and over again. "These have been some of the best years of our lives. And we'll keep in touch. Right?"

"Right, Eck," others pretty much said. "Give me a hug. And I'll call you as soon as I'm settled."

"Yeah, make sure you call. You know where to reach me,

over at Olivia's. I'm not going anywhere for a while. Hey, you remember when.....?"

It went on like this for a couple hours, until we, finally, all drifted off to our rooms. By the afternoon of the next day, everyone who was leaving was gone.

Chapter 9
Summer 2010

It's been over 38 years since the river trip and all the events surrounding it. And I'm sorry to say that, with the exception of Joe, I've lost touch with the entire Carlson staff. Suzy, Tony, Wolf, Jack, the Rev, Lisa and the rest; I have no idea what they are doing, or even if they are alive. I do, however, know a few things about some of the other characters from the Carlson scene.

Vladi, as you might have guessed, didn't stay with Wilma for very long. Nor did he stay in Chapel Hill. But unlike Alexander Solzhenitsyn, who came to the United States in 1974 to much greater fanfare than Vladi, and who subsequently retreated to the isolation of Vermont, where he criticized the U. S. for its shallow materialism; Vladi fully embraced America. In fact, Vladi thrived on shallow materialism. He soon landed in Los Angeles where he became the mass media go-to-guy for all things Russian. If you carefully check the credits on any Cold War spy movie produced up until the fall of the Soviet Union, you'll find Vladi's name in the fine print. When ABC's *Nightline* needed a commentary on anything having to deal with Soviet dissidents, Vladi was their man. In time, he became a regular on *Hollywood Squares*, happily parrying with Paul Lind, Rose Marie and the rest. And commercials! There was Vladi pitching vodka on TV, in magazines and on billboards. He was everywhere, with his personal wealth growing along with his increasing visibility. However, his muse seemingly evaporated in the L.A. sun. Vladi never published another volume of poetry. And even though his agent landed him a memoir contract with Harper and Row, the project dragged on forever and had to be completed by a ghost writer.

Naturally, this being the U. S.A., Vladi eventually learned more than he cared to about the American celebrity experience. Hollywood grew tired of him when the close of the Cold War brought a flood of fresh new Eastern European faces from the former Iron Curtain countries. The aging, overweight poet was no match for the steady stream of athletes, entrepreneurs and artists unleashed on the West. By the early nineties, Vladi, now in his sixties, was washed up and longing to return to Mother Russia.

He headed home with enough of a nest egg to maintain a comfortable, but not lavish, retirement. When I Googled Vladi's name earlier this year, there were no recent stories. The last one that I found, from 2007, was brief and had him living in a small resort somewhere along the Black Sea. His work was being rediscovered by a new generation of dissidents, twenty-somethings disgusted by Putin's reign. Reportedly, small, cadres of devoted women made pilgrimages to his seaside retreat to bask in the great man's presence. An eighty year old Vladi holding court in his bikini; the thought makes me shudder.

* * * * * *

Following his sudden departure from Carlson, I never saw Moe again. His story ended quickly and, of course, mysteriously. On May 29, 1972 in Belleville, N.J., just weeks after heading home from Chapel Hill, Moe suddenly died of an abdominal aortic aneurysm. It's rumored that his sister, Ethel, with whom he lived for the last eight years of his life, took his ashes to Israel for burial. But she never reported where. To this day, no one has found Moe Berg's final resting place.

Knowing Moe was one of the great thrills of my life. I regret that we'll never have that lunch or another long walk. I am glad, however, that he didn't kick the bucket right there in the Carlson lobby. At the time, I couldn't have handled it.

* * * * * *

I wish that I could say that Jonas went on to an outstanding career with the Tar Heels, but he didn't.   Early in his post-graduate season at HFA, he drew a flagrant foul from behind after stealing the ball at the top of the key and driving the length of the court for a layup. Jonas came down in a heap beneath the basket, writhing in pain from a severely torn knee cartilage and a torn ACL in his right leg. Today, the operation and rehab period for these injuries, while frequently season-ending, would not necessarily derail an athletic career.   But in the mid-seventies, they were bad enough to knock out even the most resilient player. Yet, the injuries didn't KO Jonas. He worked like a Spartan getting back into playing shape, spending endless hours swimming and lifting weights; then returning to the court to resume repetitions of the fast starts, stops and quick cuts demanded in basketball.

Nevertheless, after missing virtually a whole season, UNC wasn't about to take a chance on him. In fact, Jonas never fully developed into the player that he had promised to be. After the injury, he was never quite as fast or aggressive as he'd been previously been. Still, any player almost good enough to play for the Tar Heels is easily good enough to make many other NCAA Division I teams. Jonas accepted a full scholarship from the

University of New Hampshire, where he focused on his outside shooting as a two guard. He still ranks third on the school's all-time scoring list, and he would be first if the NCAA had allowed three point shots during his playing days.

After graduating in four years with a degree in Business Administration, Jonas returned to Europe to play pro ball for seven years in Spain. Late in his final season, he once again wiped out his knee, saw the handwriting on the wall, and called an end to his playing days. Today, he operates a sporting goods business in Vilnius and is the successful coach of the same Lithuanian youth club team that his father coached when Jonas was a boy. Olivia and I maintain regular email contact with Jonas; and we visited with him a few years ago when he coached the Lithuanian Junior National Team, during its tour of the U.S.

Jonas married late, at nearly 40. He and his wife have two daughters, aged 14 and 16. Both are already being scouted by women's basketball coaches at top U.S. universities. Although Jonas never got to wear his beloved Carolina Blue, perhaps his daughters will.

* * * * * *

Olivia assures me that I'm the only one who thinks so, but I'm certain that KGB survived the Haw, and that he is still alive. The river search following his alleged *drowning* never did turn up a body. To this day, he is listed as *missing and assumed dead,* rather than *deceased.* While those facts alone don't add up to a solid case, I assure you that there is more, much more.

In the mid-nineties, when Mike Tyson was attempting a comeback after serving three years in prison, I was dozing off in front of the TV while the evening sportscast was showing clips of Tyson working out at his training camp. The entire segment lasted only about 15 seconds, but I shot out of my chair when, for about 2 seconds, they showed Tyson's three body guards. There, flanked by two heavily-muscled, African American dudes, was KGB, about 20 years older with stylishly long gray hair. Still looking pretty damned fit, he held his cigarette in classic KGB fashion. Although I wasn't taping the newscast, I was able to get the video from a buddy of mine at the station.   I've reviewed it hundreds of times, and I'm certain it's him. Olivia doesn't see the resemblance. She tells me that I'm "just seeing what I want to see,"   and that the case was closed when I contacted Tyson's camp and they denied that anyone of Russian descent ever worked for Iron Mike.   Several times a year we sound like a broken record.

"Larsen, I know that you want him to be alive. Of course you do, he saved your life. I want him to be alive, too. But let's face it, he never made it out of the Haw."

"Plausible, Honey, very plausible.   But if KGB is still pinned to the bottom of the river, or if his body was somehow swept all the way out to the Atlantic, how do you explain the postcards?"

You see, every few years I get an unsigned postcard from somewhere in the U.S. Each card is from a different town or city, but they all have one thing in common; they all show the local barbecue joint. Believe me, KGB is out there, and he's still playin' with me.

* * * * * *

And Janine and Joe? Their story is the strangest of all. It's not just that they got married, stayed happily married and had four kids, now grown and on their own. Although I never would have forecast such marital bliss when we were younger and living in Carlson,   the wonder of Joe's fidelity pales in comparison to the success of his professional career. How to explain it? Where to begin? Let's return to 1972.

Immediately after graduation, Joe and I started searching for doctoral programs. For me, it wasn't such a big problem because the Communications department at UNC had a well-respected doctoral program. At such a late date, the admissions committee didn't offer me a graduate assistantship; but based on my master's degree performance, they gave me a spot in their fall, incoming class. Since UNC tuition was really cheap, student loans were easy to get, WTHL was willing to take me on part-time, and I was able to move in with Olivia; everything fell into place.

Joe had a tougher time. Recreation Administration didn't offer a Ph.D., so he had to shop around for a program, any program,that would take a chance on him. Meanwhile, he and Janine fell into a great living situation, renting a small cabin on a pond two miles east of Chapel Hill. Soon afterwards, Joe found a job waiting tables at the Rathskeller; but for months, in spite of making inquiries all over campus, it didn't look like he was going to be taking classes in September. Then, out of the blue, the chair of the Sociology department contacted him. Saying that there were two, last-minute withdrawals by incoming scholarship students, he offered Joe a tuition-free ride with a well-paying graduate assistantship requiring him to teach only one section of Introductory Sociology. To top it off, they were willing to let Joe do his dissertation work in the sociology of leisure. Suddenly, Joe was golden.

Four years later, Janine finished a second post-doctoral fellowship in Comparative Literature; and Joe was All-But-Disaertationed (ABD) in Sociology with his data, examining the density of recreational facilities in resorts along the Eastern seaboard, collected, analyzed, and almost written-up. Over the summer, he passed his dissertation defense, with high honors. In September, Janine and Joe both started teaching at UNC-

Wilmington, taking up residence in nearby Wrightsville Beach, where Joe could surf year-round.

During his fourth year at UNC-W, Joe self-published a slim book entitled *Building the Perfect Family Resort.* I bought a copy and I'm sure that his parents did too; but other than the copies that Joe gave as Christmas presents, that was about it. The book provided a line on his academic resume, but no income or prestige. And why would it? As I saw it, all that the book offered was an unimaginative set of steps for cloning Ocean City, New Jersey, using a predictable formula:

> 1) Next to a substantial body of water (ocean, lake or river), develop a *"dry"* town, shielding children from the negative influences of bars.
>
> 2) For adults, create a saloon-infested village within easy driving distance.
>
> 3) Develop a boardwalk along the waterfront of the dry town.
>
> 4) Allow enough attractions on the boardwalk to satisfy your citizens and tourists, but not so many as to make it tacky.
>
> 5) Heavily promote bicycling, water sports and other physical activities, while providing clean beaches, parks, and venues stocked with facilities (e.g. tennis, basketball and shuffleboard courts) to support residents' athletic addictions.
>
> 6) Sponsor free public concerts, an annual baby parade, a *Night-in-Venice-type* boat festival, etc., etc.

I was certain that Joe's well-worn recipe didn't have any particular audience; but suddenly, lightning struck. As the Iron Curtain crumbled, Janine translated *Building the Perfect Family Resort* into Russian, Czech, and Polish. She also seeded a few copies to colleagues around Eastern Europe. Almost instantly, the book took on a life of its own;   exploding in business and government circles within   the newly emerging capitalist economies, becoming an overnight best-seller and turning Joe into a recreational development rock star. Soon, Joe, Janine - the booster rocket who launched Joe to academic stardom - and their kids were spending summer, winter and spring vacations sojourning to Europe for Joes' steady stream of speaking engagements. His all-expense-paid trips to newly developing European resorts, along with five-figure honoraria, would have been enough; but it didn't stop there. The book was translated by enthusiasts into Chinese, Japanese and Korean, and Joe became   the toast of Asia. And finally, the international adulation led academics in the United States to reevaluate Joe's work, lauding him for the *"clarity of his vision"* and the *"elegant simplicity of his design."* In no time, his consulting fees reached six figures and the media dubbed him the *"Leisure King"* Through it all, he remained an UNC-Wilmington, where he is now Distinguished Professor of Sociology, holding the endowed Chair of Leisure Studies.

In spite of his miraculous success, Joe and I still chat on the phone, or email each other, every few weeks. Once or twice a month, he reminds me that no matter how successful he becomes, he'll never forget his roots and the little people from his past. At least some things never change.

* * * * * *

As for Olivia and me, we married midway through my doctoral program and lived in her house in Hillsborough for another twelve years. Soon after I completed my doctorate, Eric, the first of our three children, was born. Olivia continued teaching, but gave up coaching to spend time with Eric and me.

Four years later our second son, Alex, was born; followed in another four years by our daughter, Carrie. Soon after Alex's birth, Olivia cut back to teaching half-time in order to start a doctoral program in American Literature at UNC, which she completed in five years, defending her dissertation on Carrie's first birthday.

The entire time we were in Hillsborough, I failed to land a full-time, college- teaching job, but I managed to combine a half-time position at WTHL with part-time teaching at two community colleges, one in Durham and the other, west of Hillsborough, in Burlington. Even though things were tight, between Olivia's salary and mine, we were able to make ends meet. And after Olivia finished her Ph.D., we both put on a full court press in search of college jobs. It took more than a year, but Olivia eventually landed an assistant professorship in American Studies at St. Theresa College, a small, Catholic women's school in Springfield, Massachusetts. Soon afterward, I was offered an entry-level, tenure-track position in the Department of Communications at Manchester University, a 5,000 student school located about 15 miles east of Hartford, CT. Although the town of Manchester is known throughout New England for its annual Thanksgiving Day road race, rather than for its university; I was thrilled to get the job.

To split the distance on our commutes, we settled in Tarrifville, Connecticut, approximately midway between our two schools. Having three kids and two careers was a handful, but we managed to make it all work, eventually getting all three through college, while managing to remain a close family. It surely helped that we enjoyed attending almost two decades worth of kids' athletic events.

At St. Theresa, Olivia was promoted according to schedule, and within twelve years became a full professor and a department chair. Currently, she is taking a fling at administration, serving as acting Associate Vice-President for Academic Affairs. If she likes it, she might throw her hat in the ring for the position as they conduct a national search to fill it.

I travelled a bumpier professional road. While still in graduate school, I canned my dreams about launching a sports radio station after coming under the spell of a couple of young professors touting a neo-Marxist perspective called Critical Theory. Along with others in my department, I began viewing sports, especially the business side of college and professional sports, with a jaundiced eye. It's possible that Suzy's jibes about not having a serious discipline finally got to me. Perhaps knowing Moe and KGB, real spies, was a needed slap up the side of my head about life's harsher side. Or my cynicism might have been spawned by ESPN beating me to the punch, taking my sports broadcasting idea and pushing it to the max in TV, as well as radio. Whatever the cause, as ESPN – located less than an hour west of Manchester University - grew ever more successful, I became increasingly fixated on it as a prime example of capitalist excess. I seethed over it, part of the Disney Empire, exploiting sports for massive profit, while diverting the nation's attention from the far more important issues of war, poverty and environmental collapse.

When I finally earned tenure, which took me eight years and a hard fought appeal because I didn't crank out articles as quickly as my department chair wanted, I became obsessed with producing my magnum opus, a critical history of ESPN. The huge problem with this project has been that every year brings volumes more material to address. It keeps piling up like snow during a Buffalo winter. I work so hard to get on top of it; but just when I'm ready to start shutting the project down, ESPN pulls some stunt that steers me off on to yet another chapter. The other day they staged LeBron James' announcement about whether or not he would be staying in Cleveland. I mean, can you imagine anything more ridiculous?

Anyway, *the book* became a standing joke in the family and among my friends, colleagues and even my students. "Get much done on *the book* this summer, Dad?" "How's *the book* coming along, Eck?" "Nearly finished *the book*, Dr. Larsen? I'm about ready to graduate and I've been wantin' to read it since I was a freshman."

But I'll show them all. Even though not finishing *the book* has held up my promotion to full professor for years, I know that it's my destiny to finish it and that it's going to be a huge success. I hope.

* * * * * *

One weekend at the beginning of this summer, I was sitting on our back porch slaving away on *the book* and feeling frustrated about having to teach two summer school courses in order to generate some much needed cash. Olivia joined me, sat down and made a pronouncement.

"Larsen, don't make any plans for July 4th."

"Why? What do you have in mind?"

"Can't tell you."

"Why?"

"It's a surprise."

"But we don't do surprises. We've never done surprises."

"Yeah, but this is special. And you've been working too hard and worrying too much. You need a surprise"

I could tell she had her mind made up. Come hell or high water, I was going to be surprised.

When the 4th arrived, I still had no idea what Olivia had up her sleeve. All that she would tell me was that I had to help her make the food.

"The food?"

"Yep, the food."

"So, the surprise is that I get to spend all Saturday afternoon in the kitchen cooking?"

"Well, that's part of it, but there's a lot more. Trust me, a lot more."

"Ok. Point me in the right direction, and tell me what to do."

We spent the whole afternoon preparing a picnic, a really big picnic; barbecued chicken, cold cuts, homemade bread and rolls, slaw, fruit salad, three bean salad, potato salad, dip and raw vegetables, carrot cake, cookies, iced tea, lemonade, seltzer water, and two kinds of wine. It was a feast.

Eventually, I needed a break.

"Olivia, this is great, but I'm tired." I said as it was pushing 4 o'clock. "Can I take a shower and a nap before everyone shows up."

"You can take the shower, but there's not going to be any nap."

"Why not, General Patton."

"Cause nobody is coming over. We're packing the car and taking this with us."

"Where?"

"Can't tell you. That's the surprise."

"Oh for God's sake, tell me."

"Nope."

"Well, give me a hint."

"North. We're headed north on I-91."

"That's a big help."

"That's all you're going to get."

So we showered, got dressed, packed the car and made our way to the interstate, heading north to Massachusetts. I suspected that we would turn off at St. Theresa College, but Olivia told me to keep going to the Mass. Turnpike and to head west toward the Berkshires. I finally figured out our destination when she had me get off at the Lee exit and, once again, head north.

"We're going to Tanglewood, aren't we?" I smugly said, referring to the outdoor concert venue in Lenox that's the summer home of the Boston Symphony Orchestra and the Boston Pops. "So, this is my surprise. We're going to an opera, and we're going to pig out on a week's worth of food."

"Wrong!" Olivia said in mock exasperation. "Just keep driving. You'll see."

Although I had the destination, I remained clueless as we moved along the winding drive to picturesque Lenox and beyond to the concert cite. Even as we parked the car some distance from the entrance and then hauled two packed coolers - on rollers, a blanket and a couple of lawn chairs towards the gate; I didn't know what was in store for us. Then the posters at the ticket booth appeared.

"Whoa! James Taylor and Carole King. I didn't know they were coming here. This is a surprise, a really cool surprise. Thanks."

"You're welcome. I got the tickets six months ago."

"And you never told me."

"Nope."

"But what if I had gone ahead and planned something else for us?

"You wouldn't have done anything without checking with me. And besides, you've had your head so caught up in ESPN and *the book* that you weren't going to plan anything fun. A decade could go by without you planning anything fun. That's why I always do it."

"Ouch," I said, feeling suitably chastised. "But who is all the food for?"

"You'll see. Let's go find our spot on the lawn."

The place was packed, but with a very mellow feeling as young people and older folks, like us, mingled while anticipating a great concert in the gentle, evening breezes of the Berkshires. After about ten minutes of stumbling around, and over, others who already had their picnic locations staked out, I begged, "Olivia, do you have any idea where we're going? Can we just park ourselves here?"

"Of course. We've arrived, Larsen." Olivia declared. "Look right in front of you."

As I glanced around, there were the smiling faces of our son, Eric, with his girlfriend, Kirsten; our daughter, Carrie, with her boyfriend, Patrick; and our younger son, Alex, with his girlfriend, Nora.

"Hey, the whole gang is here! Nice planning, Olivia. Very nicely done."

"Now look behind you."

As I turned, I heard a familiar, somewhat irritating and completely unexpected voice say, " I didn't think that you were ever going to get here, Big Guy. What took you so long?"

"Joe, what are you doing here? And Janine, thank God you're with him. At least, it's really great to see you."

"Oh, give me some love, Eck," the now fully gray Leisure King said as he wrapped his arms around me in a bear hug. "I've been through hell for six months with Olivia constantly hounding me about being here on time. And it cost us a small fortune to fly from Wilmington to Hartford; but you know me. I spare no expense when it comes to those who helped me along the way. And now we're here. We've finally made it. The long journey is over. Let the party begin."

And party we did; throughout the evening. Although they had aged along with us, James Taylor was as amiable, strong and self-effacing as ever; and Carole King was still remarkably sassy and powerful. Performing most of their memorable hits, accompanied by an exceptional troupe of vocalists and musicians; they delivered *Sweet Baby James, Shower the People, Fire and Rain, Way Over Yonder, Sweet Seasons, Natural Woman* and many more. It was fantastic.

Then, late in the concert, James broke into *Carolina in My Mind*.

"Wow!" I thought. "That's what was on my VW radio when Joe and I first saw Vladi and Janine."

For years, I hadn't given much, if any, thought to all of the people in Carlson and the trip down the Haw. But in that moment, it all came rushing back to me.